MARRYING MAX

Max Richardson was looking for a suitable home to live in with his niece, Emily, whilst her parents sorted out their marriage. Under pressure, he realised that Thea Sinclair's eccentric house would have to do — but he had misgivings. Then, when he and Thea had to pretend they were engaged, it caused them both emotional turmoil. Thea wanted marriage and children, but Max wouldn't risk commitment — and you can't just pretend to be in love . . .

NELL DIXON

MARRYING MAX

Complete and Unabridged

LINFORD
Leicester

Gloucestershire County Council	

British Library CIP Data

Dixon, Nell
    Marrying Max.—Large print ed.—
Linford romance library
1. Love stories
2. Large type books
I. Title
823.9′2 [F]

ISBN 978–1–84617–680–7

Published by
F. A. Thorpe (Publishing)
Anstey, Leicestershire

Set by Words & Graphics Ltd.
Anstey, Leicestershire
Printed and bound in Great Britain by
T. J. International Ltd., Padstow, Cornwall

This book is printed on acid-free paper

A Horrible Mistake

Max stared at the house then glanced back down at the sheet of paper in his hand. He couldn't possibly be in the right place.

'The house itself is an architectural gem, offering the perfect family environment.' He read the letter from Ginny, his former secretary, out loud in disbelief and looked up once more at the façade in front of him. 'This is never going to work.'

Stone gargoyles peered down from their ledges and nooks. Curves and curly fascia boards with peeling paint sat on top of the bright red bricks like melted icing on a particularly ugly cake.

Max shook his head. 'All this place needs is some bats around the turret and a storm cloud on top!'

Right on cue, the dark grey sky which had been threatening rain all morning decided to oblige.

What on earth had Ginny been thinking of when she had suggested this place as a suitable home for his niece? Even if Thea Sinclair was the Mary Poppins-like paragon of virtue Ginny had kept boasting about, there was no way his sister was going to allow him to bring his little niece, Emily, to live here.

Convinced he was wasting his time, he tugged impatiently on the large brass angel bell next to the front door.

No one appeared from inside to answer the unmelodious clanking.

Stepping back a pace, he surveyed the blank windows. The house appeared empty; Ginny's friend had obviously forgotten he was coming.

The summer shower was rapidly developing into a fully-fledged downpour as, annoyed at having driven so far in vain, he turned towards his car.

At that a small boy in shorts and a T-shirt raced round the corner of the building and cannoned into Max's legs.

'Can you come and help Thea? She's stuck!'

Bemused, Max followed his young guide around the corner to a sash window on the side of the house. A pair of damp, denim-clad legs waved wildly in the air as their owner attempted to free herself from the weight of the frame. The sash had closed firmly on her bottom, trapping her half in and half out of the window.

Max addressed the rain-soaked bottom; the rest of its owner was inside the house. 'Are you trying to break in or get out?'

A muffled reply and more agitated leg waving answered him.

'The window blew the door shut and we got locked out,' explained the small boy helpfully. 'Thea thought she could squeeze in through the study window but the frame slid down and her bum's too big. I'm Tom. I live next door.'

Max groaned. He should have recognised Tom from the hundreds of photographs Ginny had shown him when they had met at his office last week. So this house was indeed Stony Gables and presumably this must be the bottom half of his hostess.

He seized the sash and managed to pull it upwards a little so the weight of the frame was off the woman's back. Immediately the legs disappeared inside the house with a crash and an agonised shriek.

'Are you all right?' He tried peering inside through the glass but couldn't make anything out in the gloom. Rainwater was dripping off his hair and the end of his nose. What had started out as a fine summer's day was quickly turning into a cold, wet one and he was soaked to the skin.

'I'm fine. Come round — I'll open the front door,' a disembodied female voice called. Max couldn't see where she had gone.

'You're very wet,' Tom observed.

'So are you,' Max replied grimly and followed his little helper back around to the front of the house.

The young woman waiting to greet them on the step was not the cardigan-wearing, middle-aged spinster he had pictured from his chat with Ginny. Instead Theodora Sinclair appeared to be a slender young woman who, in addition to possessing shapely denim-clad legs, also had a cloud of wild blonde curls and silver toe-rings on her bare feet.

Thea surveyed the two dripping wet people in front of her with dismay. So much for her carefully planned welcome! She thought ruefully about the sedate new summer dress she had hanging upstairs in her bedroom. The wet and cross-looking man in front of her would never want to stay here or hire her to help him care for his niece now.

It was typical of her luck to mess things up, and besides all that, her knees hurt from where she had crash-landed on to the study floor.

'Come in, I'll find some towels. Tom, go through to the kitchen.' Biting her lip in despair, she ushered them both inside. 'I'm so sorry about this.'

She bustled around the large old-fashioned kitchen, pulling towels from the wooden airer in the scullery. 'Tom followed me outside and a gust of wind caught the door.' She peeped at the stern face of the sodden man in her kitchen. Perhaps he would see the funny side. 'I forgot that the sash weights in the study window aren't balanced right,' she went on. 'Every now and then it slides itself shut. I must have knocked it when I climbed through.' She blinked at him, looking hopefully for a glimmer of understanding. 'Could happen to anybody.' She laughed nervously.

'Shut up, Thea,' she told herself. Her guest wasn't smiling.

'It happens to you a lot, Thea,' Tom added helpfully. 'Like when you fell off the veranda roof rescuing Action Man's parachute and when Mum's geese got out and chased you.'

She hastily enveloped Tom's head in

a towel and began to rub vigorously at his short spiky hair.

'I'm sorry, I haven't introduced myself properly — I'm Theodora Sinclair. And I presume you must be . . . ?'

The formidable man paused in his drying to say, 'Max Richardson.'

So it *was* him. Her last wild hope that he might have been a passing double-glazing salesman died.

'I take it you were expecting me today?' He didn't sound very sympathetic about her mishap with the door and the window.

'Yes, Ginny said you'd be here about eleven. Everything's all ready.'

He lifted one dark eyebrow as if he questioned this assurance.

Peeling off his wet shirt, he draped it over the back of one of the scrubbed pine kitchen chairs.

Thea knew she was staring at the well-developed muscles of his chest. Ginny had said her former boss was good-looking but she hadn't said *how* good. Only when his hands moved to the waistband of his trousers did Thea manage to utter a squeak of protest. He couldn't!

Frowning, Max fumbled in his pocket and pulled out a set of car keys which he tossed over to her. 'Would you mind getting my holdall from the boot of the car? I'm freezing.'

Flustered, she watched, horrified, as he unzipped. *He was!*

'Are you going to take your pants off, too?' Tom enquired innocently from his cosy cocoon of towels. Without waiting to hear the reply, Thea grabbed the keys and fled crimson-faced into the rain towards Max's gleaming silver Mercedes.

Tom watched with avid interest as Max dropped the saturated trousers on to the tabletop and wrapped a large towel around his waist over his boxer shorts.

'Thea's face was all pink,' Tom observed. 'Did you know you could ask your mummy to buy you pants with pictures on them?'

Max sighed; Ginny, whilst more tactful, was just as plain speaking and her son clearly took after her.

'Would you like a biscuit?' Tom pointed at a tea-tray on the dresser, which was all set out ready with cups and a plate of cookies. 'Thea bought chocolate ones specially. Mummy told her you like them.'

'Mummy seems to have said quite a lot of things,' Max observed dryly.

Tom helped himself to the cookies. 'Thea's not very good with cars. She only drives a bike. Do you like bikes?'

Thea came panting back into the kitchen. 'I had a bit of trouble with the key,' she said as she proffered him the large navy holdall.

Tom looked at Max meaningfully as if to say, 'See? I told you,' and popped another biscuit in his mouth.

'No biscuits, not before lunch!' Thea dived to cover the half-empty plate and glared at the unrepentant Tom.

'Would you like a cup of tea or

coffee?' she asked Max, a flustered expression still on her face.

'Thanks, but if you could show me to my room I'd like to get some clothes on first.' Once he had some dry clothes on he would be able to make his excuses and escape from this mad house.

'Oh yes, of course. I'll take you upstairs.' Her face was now as pink as her T-shirt and she scuttled into the hall and up the carved wooden staircase like a startled rabbit.

★　★　★

The house was as eccentric on the inside as it was on the outside. A great stuffed grizzly bear wearing a tie and a panama hat stood next to the grandfather clock in the tiled hallway, and at the top of the landing a wall-painting gave the impression that you were entering through a stone archway into open countryside.

'I thought you might like the Blue Room,' Thea was saying as she led the way, 'and then your niece could have the little bedroom in the tower. It's the next door down. It was my room when I was small. It's perfect for a little girl.'

She opened a white panelled door and Max stared. He could see why it was called the Blue Room. Walls, ceilings, curtains, carpet, even the hangings on the carved oak four-poster bed which dominated the room, were all blue.

'There's a nice view of the garden.' Thea had crossed over to the large sash window, which had a window seat in the deep bay. 'And there's a door through here into the bathroom.' She led the way over to another door and flung it open.

Max peered inside to discover an enormous claw-footed cast iron bath amidst the rest of the Victorian plumbing. He thought longingly of the power shower and streamlined minimalism of his warehouse conversion flat.

'It all looks lovely, thank you.' He

struggled to be polite; his hostess had clearly tried to make the room look inviting with fresh towels and a posy of flowers.

Thea looked relieved, her face lighting up at his praise.

'I'll leave you to get changed and I'll go and put the kettle on.'

The door clicked shut behind her and Max sank down on the edge of the bed.

Glumly he surveyed his surroundings. Stony Gables had sounded like such a good idea when Ginny had suggested it. She could normally be relied upon to show good judgment, and finding a suitable family home for rent which was owned by a nursery teacher in need of a temporary job was a miracle indeed. For his niece's sake, he had to make the arrangement with Thea work somehow, for he was rapidly running out of time and options.

Pulling on dry jeans, his mind ran back over the last conversation he'd had with his younger sister.

'She can't stay with you! It's ridiculous, **Max**. I know you love Emily and she'd be happy, but you have no idea how to care for a child her age twenty-four hours a day.'

'But, Julia, you've admitted she'd be happier staying with me rather than with Great-Aunt Nettie while you're away.' He had tried to reason with her. Julia and Paul's marriage was degenerating into a war zone and Emily was caught up in the no-man's-land in the middle.

'Where would she sleep? Who would care for her while you're at work?' His sister had rounded on him fiercely. 'You can't have a little girl sleeping in that one-bedroomed museum of a flat of yours — and don't tell me that my child is going to be cared for by a stream of your girlfriends. It would be different if you were settled or had a house.'

Max was forced to concede some of her argument.

'What if I rent a house? A nice family home? I'll work partly from there and

13

take time off. I can engage a proper nanny for Emily so she'll be well cared for. She'd love it, Julia; it would be like a real holiday.'

He had waited with bated breath for her response. Julia's husband was being transferred abroad with his job for the next eight weeks and Julia intended to use the time travelling with him to try to resolve their marriage problems.

'I don't know, Max, it's expecting a lot of you. I mean, you're hardly Mr Commitment.'

However, he had sensed she was wavering and pressed ahead with his case. 'At least let me find somewhere and you can have a look. You aren't due to leave for a few weeks yet. It's got to be better than Emily staying with Aunt Nettie.'

Eventually, after much persuasion, she agreed, which was why he was now here at Stony Gables.

He sighed. Seeing Emily suffer while her parents bickered in front of her like two dogs with a bone reminded him of his own childhood only too well. Ten years older than Julia, he remembered vividly the nights he had spent sitting on the stairs with his arm around his baby sister, comforting her while their parents fought. He couldn't bear to see little Emily have to go through the same thing alone.

★   ★   ★

Thea could hear Tom's clear voice as she walked back downstairs and she automatically speeded up. If he had answered the door after everything she had told him about talking to strangers . . .

' . . . I'll strangle the little monkey,' she muttered.

To her relief, it was Tom's mother's light laughter she could hear. Ginny smiled as Thea entered the room.

'Tom told me you'd gone upstairs with a man who was only wearing his pants!'

Tom grinned innocently at Thea

from his chair by the Aga, a ring of chocolate round his mouth.

Thea explained what had happened while she made a pot of tea.

Ginny smiled ruefully and shook her head. 'Oh, Thea! I thought we had it all planned so beautifully. Trust you to muck it up!'

'I can't help it. Things just happen to me.' She leaned comfortably on the rail fronting the Aga and took a sip of her tea.

'I see you didn't change your clothes, either.' Ginny frowned disapprovingly at Thea's tatty jeans and midriff-revealing T-shirt.

'I was going to, honestly. I just hadn't anticipated getting wedged in a window.' She caught Ginny's eye and burst out laughing, and though her friend tried to look cross, she failed miserably and was soon giggling too.

'You are hopeless, Thea. You need this job, remember? Your new post at the day nursery doesn't start till September and you have to get the repairs done to this place if you want to stay here.'

Thea sobered. 'I know — and I am grateful for everything you've done for me, Ginny.' Ginny would never know how much Thea appreciated the help and support she had given her during her father's long illness.

The kitchen door squeaked open and Ginny turned to smile a welcome. 'Max! How lovely to see you. Thea was just telling me about her mishap.'

Max bent to kiss Ginny's cheek. 'I gathered that from the laughter I heard on the stairs,' he remarked dryly. He still didn't appear to have found the situation funny.

Thea busied herself with the teapot, her hands trembling. 'I made you a cup of tea; help yourself to sugar and cookies . . . ' Her voice trailed off as she noticed the empty plate and the wide-eyed expression on Tom's face.

Ginny intercepted the look and stood up. 'Oh, boy, it's time we went. Come on, Tom, you've annoyed Thea long enough for today. Thanks for looking after him, Thea. I'll leave you two to talk and to make all the arrangements for Emily's stay.' As she spoke, she hauled her son out of his comfy chair, shoved his freshly-dried clothes back on him and marched him out of the door.

That left Max and Thea.

She gestured for him to take a seat and looked at him warily. 'So — Ginny said you're interested in renting the house for a short time and in employing me as housekeeper and nanny for your little niece?'

It was hard to tell what he was thinking. He didn't look any less intimidating in jeans and a casual top than he had when she had opened the front door to see him standing there in his designer shirt and trousers.

Guiltily she hoped nothing bad would happen to them while they dried out on the top of the Aga. She had melted all the buttons on a brand new top a few weeks ago when she had put it on the hot plate by mistake.

'I'm not sure how much Ginny has told you about the circumstances, Miss Sinclair, but my niece has been having a difficult time lately and I'm looking for a home with a nice family atmosphere while her parents are away.' He seemed to be picking his words carefully.

'Stony Gables would be perfect then,' Thea jumped in eagerly. 'This is a lovely family home and I'm sure you'd both be comfortable here. There's a neighbour's pony in the field at the bottom of the garden and lots of room to play. And I have a study off the lounge, which you can use to work from.'

'I'm sure you love your home very much, Miss Sinclair, but I'm not sure it's quite . . . ' He tailed off, looking a little uncomfortable.

'Oh, please, call me Thea. I'm a very good cook, too — and I'm a trained nursery teacher, so your niece would be in good hands while you were at work.'

In her eagerness to convince him she wiggled forward to the edge of her chair, slopping a little of her tea on to the tabletop. She willed him mentally to say yes and agree to employ her while she tried to hide the puddle of tea with her mug.

'Miss Sinclair — Thea — I'm sure you have glowing references and Ginny has sung your praises to the rafters — '

'But?' There had to be a but, she could tell. Perhaps her house was too old and shabby for him. Judging by his clothes and the fancy car outside, she knew he must be used to the best of everything.

Her heart sank; she had been counting on the income his stay would bring.

He paused and appeared to be weighing his words with care. 'You have a seven-foot-tall stuffed grizzly bear wearing a tie and a hat in your hall.'

She stared at him. What kind of criticism was that?

'My sister is being very particular about the arrangements she makes for Emily. She leaves for the Far East in less than two weeks, so I haven't much time left to find a suitable home. I'd already been looking for quite a while when Ginny suggested here.'

Thea frowned. What was he trying to say? That he didn't like her house but didn't have much choice left? That was what it sounded like.

She bristled defensively. 'My home may be old, Mr Richardson, but you'll see it's very clean and comfortable. I'm sure your sister will be quite happy to leave Emily here when she goes away with her husband.'

'Please, call me Max,' he conceded. 'It's very important to me that Julia does decide to trust me with Emily's care. The only other viable arrangement is that she stays with her father's elderly great-aunt, who is very kind and well-meaning but is also extremely deaf and has a large moustache. Emily is terrified of her.'

Thea sighed and rested her elbows on the table. 'Ginny said your home isn't suitable for Emily to stay there?'

He nodded and took a sip of his tea. 'It's a one-bedroomed apartment in a warehouse conversion in the centre of the city.'

'And there's no Mrs Richardson or future Mrs Richardson to help you with Emily?' She met his gaze squarely. She hadn't noticed a ring.

'No, and nor is there likely to be,' he declared vehemently. 'I don't believe in marriage.'

Thea wondered briefly what had happened in his life to make him so cynical. Unless — had he thought she was asking out of personal interest? He had a big opinion of himself if that was the case!

'Well, I'd better show you around so you can think about things,' she suggested.

Feeling decidedly nettled, she rose and carried her empty mug over to the sink, glad of an opportunity to allow her hot cheeks to cool. Rinsing her mug and standing it on the draining board, she noticed the peeling paint on the window frame as if through fresh eyes. Critical eyes.

She had to convince Max that Stony Gables would be a good home for Emily. She needed the money his rent and her wages would bring. It would mean she could get the house painted and the heating fixed, the plumbing redone and the roof repaired . . .

She allowed herself a blissful little daydream of all the things she could do with the cash, before squashing her little fantasy flat. There was no point in thinking about all her plans if it looked like he was going to say, 'Thanks but no thanks' and go on his way.

★ ★ ★

Some forty minutes later, having toured the house from attics to cellar, Max found himself standing rather dazedly back in the kitchen where they had started. Thea had talked non-stop on her tour and that, combined with the fact this was the oddest house he had ever been in, made him feel more than a little disorientated.

He had to admit that the house had a quirky charm though. In many ways it was much better than any of the other properties he had seen. He had scrutinised Thea's references before leaving London, so he knew there was no problem there, plus Ginny had recommended her very highly.

She was smiling at him expectantly, her long silver earrings swinging as she awaited a response to the question she had apparently just asked.

'I'm sorry, I was thinking. What did you say?'

She smiled. 'I asked if you would like some lunch.'

'Yes, thank you.' He sat down at the table while she buzzed about the kitchen, humming softly to herself.

While she busied herself preparing a meal, he tried to pin down why he was so reluctant to admit to himself that this house would make a good home for himself and Emily. Thea was a pretty young woman, but definitely not his type. So why did he find her long slim legs and wild hair so attractive? His tastes ran more to elegant brunettes like Gabby, his last girlfriend.

But would Julia be happy to entrust Emily's care to someone as scatter-brained as Thea appeared to be? She might be well-qualified with lots of experience — Ginny certainly trusted her with her beloved Tom — but from her rambling conversation, she seemed to be as eccentric as her home.

'Here we are.' She slid a large plate of salad and quiche in front of him. 'Would you like a glass of wine?'

'Yes, thanks. This looks very nice. Did you make the quiche yourself?'

She poured him a glass of white wine. 'Yes, and I grew the salad stuffs and made the bread. I grow a lot of my own things. It's healthier.'

She sat down opposite him and began to eat, her silver-blonde curls luminous around her small face.

'So how long have you been renting

out rooms here?' he wondered. 'Ginny said you normally do bed and breakfast for business travellers?'

She nodded, her long earrings twinkling in the light from the window. 'I moved back here twelve months ago to care for my father while he was ill. I needed to be with him twenty-four hours a day, so I gave up my job and my flat to come home.' A shadow passed over her face. 'After he died, I inherited Stony Gables — and a heap of debt. I used my savings to pay off as much as I could and I got a few repairs done on the house. I've a new job lined up in the autumn at the local nursery school, but in the meantime the B and B business helps pay the bills.'

He sipped his wine and regarded her thoughtfully. There was evidently more to her than he had originally thought. He wondered if she had given up some man as well as her home and career.

Irritated by the direction his thoughts were taking, he forced himself back on track.

'It must be quite difficult living in a house this size on your own. You've never thought of selling it and buying something smaller?'

It seemed to him the logical thing to do. A house this size was plainly going to need far more upkeep than a young, single nursery teacher could provide.

She laughed, her blue eyes sparkling. 'Sell Stony Gables? Never! Mind you, the estate agent in the village keeps trying to persuade me.'

'This house means a lot to you then?' He smiled; he couldn't imagine anyone being sentimental about a piece of property. His youth had taught him that nothing was for ever, so there was no point in becoming attached to anything or anyone.

'Of course.' Thea stared at him, her eyes as round with astonishment as Tom's had been earlier when she had confiscated the cookies. 'This is my home. My great-grandfather had this house built to his own design.' Sipping her wine, she added, 'I had such a happy childhood here, I know Emily is going to love it.'

He sighed. 'I hope so. Right now Emily could do with a nice period of uncomplicated childhood.' A pang of envy shot through him. If only his and Julia's childhood had been as idyllic.

Thea's expressive blue eyes warmed with concern. 'When do you expect her to come and visit?'

'I'll ask Julia and Emily to come down tomorrow. Paul's already left for Singapore so it's all up to Julia to finalise the arrangements for Emily. I just have to phone her and confirm the arrangements. If she approves then we'll go ahead with the rental agreement.' Unexpectedly he felt reassured by Thea's ready sympathy for Emily's situation.

She stood up and began to clear the plates. 'In that case, I'll prepare a room later for your sister to stay in while she's here.'

Watching her stack the crockery, Max hoped he was doing the right thing. He had to persuade Julia that he was more than capable of caring for Emily. He just had to pray that Thea and Stony Gables would manage to work their quirky charm on his stubborn and single-minded sister.

'We're Engaged!'

After lunch, Thea tidied up the kitchen and folded the laundry while Max went off to the study to telephone his sister and confirm the arrangements for her visit.

It felt a little strange having Max in the house. Her other bed and breakfast clients had been business people who had arrived in time for a late supper, retired to their rooms with their laptops, emerged in the morning to eat a hearty breakfast, and had then departed.

She hoped she wouldn't regret the arrangement with Max. It had sounded perfect when Ginny had suggested it as the ideal solution to both their problems, but having Max around was subtly disturbing to her senses. She hadn't spent this much time in close proximity on her own with a man since her ex-boyfriend, Jon, and that particular memory didn't please her at all.

She sighed, absentmindedly twisting her bracelets around on her wrist. If only her father had left a little money to help with the upkeep on Stony Gables, then she wouldn't need to have strangers in her home.

'And if wishes were horses then beggars would ride.' She laughed out loud, remembering one of her father's favourite phrases, but her smile faded as she recalled the last few traumatic months of his illness.

She tried to look on the bright side: at least having Max here was only going to be for a short time, and she was looking forward to meeting Emily. She loved children; it was why she had gone into teaching as a career.

She smiled to herself. She looked forward to the day when she could have her own children running around Stony Gables and hoped she could give them the same kind of loving childhood she had enjoyed. The money Max was offering to pay her as a salary together with the sum he had assured her was the market rate for renting a property similar to hers would help bring her dreams one step closer to reality by enabling her to stay in her home.

The insistent ringing of the telephone jolted her out of her reverie.

'Thea, I forgot to remind you and Max about tonight. You are both still coming to dinner, aren't you?' Ginny's voice sounded distracted.

'Well, I can't speak for Max, but yes, of course I'm coming.' Thea felt guilty; in all the excitement of the day she had forgotten about her friend's dinner party. The invitation had been issued a week ago when Max had first arranged to visit Stony Gables.

'I know Max won't have forgotten,' Ginny declared confidently. 'Only I need a bit of moral support. Laurence has invited most of the local great and good. He really wants to build up some support before he raises the subject of relocating the surgery.'

Thea grinned. Ginny's husband Laurence, the local GP, had the power to lure the birds from the trees. She was sure that was where Tom had inherited a large part of his charm.

'I promise I'll be there.'

'On time?' Ginny enquired wryly, and Thea laughed. She had been half an hour late for her friend's last dinner party, arriving after everyone had finished the soup, thanks to a puncture in her bike tyre on her way over.

'I promise. I'll even wear a dress and posh up.'

Ginny laughed. 'OK, you're off the hook. At least Max can bring you in his car tonight so we'll be spared the sight of you covered in bike oil!'

Thea chuckled at her good-natured teasing, before going to tell Max about the phone call and to pass on Ginny's reminder.

He was busy in the study setting up his laptop on her father's old cherry wood desk. She tapped hesitantly on the half-open door, scolding herself for feeling like an intruder in her own home.

'Ginny just rang to see if we're still going to her dinner party tonight.'

He looked up from the computer, frowning slightly as if he didn't have a clue what she was talking about.

'You are still going, aren't you?' she pressed. 'Ginny seemed certain you were. Tonight's really important to her and Laurence. I thinks she's counting on us for moral support.'

'Oh — yes, of course.' He smiled and her breath caught in her throat at the sudden change in his features. He looked so different when he smiled, younger and less severe. Intuitively she knew this man was carrying an awful lot of emotional baggage and if she were wise she would steer clear. The trouble was, she had never been wise when it came to her fellow human beings and their problems.

'Thea's lame ducks.' She heard her father's voice as clearly as if he were standing beside her. The number of times she had turned up with a person or animal and their tale of woe. She smiled a little at the memory.

'I — er, I'll leave you to it then. Help yourself to tea or coffee. If you want anything I'll be in the garden.'

*   *   *

Max waited till Thea had left the room and then pushed the laptop away from him with a sigh. He didn't feel at all like going out to a dinner party this evening and socialising with a group of people he didn't know.

Interlocking his fingers, he placed his hands behind his head and leaned back in the chair. Looking out through the window, he realised it was the same one he had freed Thea from only a few hours earlier. The room itself was pleasant and well proportioned but decorated in the same eclectic and eccentric style that characterised the rest of the house.

The white Adam-style fireplace had a

collection of shells, feathers and tiny fairy dolls on the mantelpiece. The bookshelves were crammed with photographs and trinkets as well as books. Most of the photographs were of Thea as a little girl; smiling at the seaside, skipping in the garden, eating an ice-cream at a fair. Others showed her with her parents, grinning confidently at the camera. The later pictures just had Thea alone or with her father. Max wondered what had happened to her mother.

The conversation with Julia a few minutes earlier hadn't gone well. She had seemed preoccupied with joining Paul in Singapore and appeared unconvinced that the arrangements Max had made for Emily would work. In desperation, he had fudged the truth a little in an attempt to convince her.

'Thea's house is perfect for Emily, Julia. She's a nursery teacher and really good with kids.'

'I'm sure she is, but it's you I'm more concerned about. How do I know that the minute I'm on that plane you won't be rushing back off to the city and Gabby or one of the other women you might be seeing?'

Max had bitten his tongue at the implication in his sister's tone that he was some kind of irresponsible womaniser.

'Thea is a very special person and I love Emily,' he had cajoled. 'I'd never make an arrangement involving her that wouldn't work.'

His sister had latched on to just the first six words in his sentence: 'Thea is a very special person.'

'Wait, does this mean you've met a woman who might settle down with you at last?' The tone of her voice had changed and in a weak moment Max had blurred the truth. Suddenly after a few more questions, she had seemed much more willing to bring Emily to Stony Gables.

The snag was, she now thought there was a relationship between himself and Thea. Why was nothing in life simple?

What difference did it make to the arrangements for Emily anyway? He would never for the life of him be able to understand women.

Thinking furiously, he drew the laptop towards him. Once he had got his work sorted out he would go and find Thea and inform her of the extra request he now had for his stay at Stony Gables.

★　★　★

Thea was surprised to see Max coming down the path towards her vegetable garden, carrying two mugs of tea. Immersed in her weeding while the ground was still soft, she had temporarily forgotten she had a guest.

'I thought you might like a cup of tea,' he announced. 'That looks like thirsty work.' He nodded at the half-filled barrow of weeds.

Straightening up, she wiped her muddy hands on the back of her jeans and took the drink from him gratefully.

'Mmm, the warm weather and the rain showers have made everything shoot up. Did you get your computer all set up?'

'Yes, no problems at all. Thank you.'

Thea looked down at her grimy hands and nails. 'I'd better finish off soon and try to clean up if I'm to look respectable for tonight.'

Max followed her gaze. 'I don't suppose there's a manicurist around here, is there?' he teased.

'D.I.Y. only,' she said, laughing, and swallowed the last of her tea.

Max took the empty mug from her and, expecting him to go back up to the house, she grasped the handles of the wheelbarrow, ready to move her load to the compost heap. But he appeared to be rooted to the spot.

She looked at him quizzically. 'Did you want something?'

He scratched the back of his head, a faintly embarrassed expression on his face. 'I — er — spoke to my sister earlier.'

Warily Thea set down the handles of the barrow.

'Was everything all right?'

Max looked sheepish and was strangely reluctant to meet her gaze.

'Fine. That is, she's still coming, and she seems happier about leaving Emily with me now, but . . . ' He broke off with a forceful sigh, and looked directly at her. 'It's just she — and I swear it wasn't really anything I said — but she thinks we're a couple.'

Thea knew she was staring but her brain was struggling to take in what he had just said.

'What do you mean, she thinks we're a couple? How can it not be something you said?'

'I said you were a really nice person and she took it the wrong way.'

'Then why didn't you put her right?'

Max was squirming like a fish on a hook. He reminded her of Tom when he had been caught out doing something he shouldn't.

'I should have, I know, and I'm sorry.

But she was so much happier about Emily staying here when she thought you and I were engaged.'

'Engaged!' The word came out as an incredulous squeak. Thea sank down on the low stone wall which bordered the vegetable garden. 'If Ginny hadn't vouched for you I would swear you were insane! You let your sister believe we're not only a couple but that we're engaged?'

He sat down on the wall next to her. 'I'm sorry. But Emily so much needs some stability at the moment, and Julia was never entirely happy about her staying with me.' He shifted uncomfortably. 'It's my own fault in a way. Julia and I had such a miserable childhood. Our parents fought constantly and used us as the weapons to play off each other.'

A dull red flush crept above the collar of his shirt and he dug his thumbnail into a clump of moss on the coping stone.

'I told you earlier, I don't believe in

marriage. I would never want a child of mine to go through what I went through. That's why, when I see Emily suffering, I just want to protect her while Julia and Paul sort themselves out.' He shot her a sidelong glance, clearly uncomfortable at sharing so much with a virtual stranger. 'I don't have a good longevity record with relationships. I don't want anything permanent or serious. Julia thinks this means I don't have the commitment needed to care for Emily while she's away.'

'And do you?' Thea pressed. 'Do you have the commitment?'

His dark brown eyes met hers for a long moment and her pulse speeded up while her face warmed under the intensity of his gaze.

'I'll do whatever it takes to make Emily happy.'

'Even lie to her mother?' Thea questioned softly.

His face clouded and he stood up abruptly. 'You're right. I don't know what I was thinking. When she gets here I'll tell her the truth.'

He turned on his heel and marched back towards the house.

Thea sighed and grasped the wheelbarrow handles again. Today certainly wasn't turning out to be one of your average days. It wasn't every day you got engaged and then dumped by a virtual stranger all before the six o'clock news.

Max strode back up the path leading to the house. What had he been thinking? The engagement idea was crazy. Why would Thea want to go along with it? She was right, of course, about lying to Julia. Yet in the circumstances it had seemed such a harmless deception to allow his sister to think there was more to his renting Thea's home than just a business arrangement.

The difficulty now was, how was it all going to affect Emily? He would just have to try his best to persuade Julia when she arrived that he was still the best person to leave Emily with. His heart sank; it would be an almost impossible task once he confessed the truth.

As he rinsed the mugs under the kitchen tap, he glanced through the window to see Thea coming along the path, her wild hair blowing in the light breeze that had sprung up from nowhere. Her jeans were covered in streaks of mud and her T-shirt had riden up, exposing her slender, flat stomach. He swallowed. Thea Sinclair was a very attractive young woman; it wouldn't have been any hardship to pretend he was engaged to her.

Thea felt Max watching her even before she reached the back door. She paused on the step, conscious for once of her untidy and grubby appearance. Hastily she ran her hands through her wayward hair. What must he think of her?

She kicked off her muddy sandals outside the back door and went through into the scullery to wash her hands.

'I want to apologise. I don't know what I was thinking.' Max was leaning on the doorframe between the two rooms.

A twinge of pity pulled at her conscience. He looked so downcast.

'That's OK,' she assured him. 'I know you were only thinking of Emily. I'm sure Julia will see it was just a misunderstanding.'

'What time do we have to be at Ginny's?' He changed the subject quickly, clearly regretting his earlier confidences.

'Half seven for drinks, eating at eight. I don't know how many people she's invited.' Thea looked at her nails and groaned. 'I suppose I'd better do some emergency work on my hands. Ginny wants to make a good impression tonight.'

'She said something about Laurence relocating his surgery?' Max stood back politely from the doorframe to allow her to pass through.

'Yes, I think a few people complained

about the plans so Laurence wants to get as many influential people on his side as he can. He really needs a bigger building; they're so cramped where they are.' She paused by the hall door. 'I'd better go and start to get ready. I'll see you later.'

★   ★   ★

Max was waiting for her in the lounge when she came back downstairs. He looked amazingly tall, dark and debonair rising out of her shabby chintz armchair as she entered the room.

'You look very lovely, Thea.' There was genuine admiration in his tone and she felt a rosy glow of pleasure at his praise.

She had made a special effort for tonight, telling herself it was for Ginny, although a tiny bit of her admitted that it was sheer feminine vanity to show Max that she could look good. The dress was one of her favourites, a soft, filmy material in a delicate floral print

46

with a jagged hemline. She had left her hair loose, just pinning up the sides with a couple of flowery clips.

'You don't look so bad yourself,' she said lightly, and cringed at how naff she sounded. Boy, was she out of practice at this dating stuff!

He smiled at her. 'Your coach awaits then, Cinders — but you'll have to direct me. I know Tom said he was next-door but I gather that means a few miles down the road.'

He offered her his arm and, suddenly feeling a little shy, she picked up her bag from the table and cautiously accepted.

Max's car was as luxurious on the inside as it had looked from the outside. Sliding into the passenger seat and attempting to look graceful, Thea blushed as she remembered how she had struggled to work the key fob earlier in the day.

'Tom told me that you ride a bike. He didn't say if it's a motorbike or a cycle,' Max said conversationally as he started the engine.

'Cycle,' she replied promptly as they pulled away. 'I don't think I'd be very safe on a motorbike.'

He flashed a smile at her. 'From some of the things Tom was telling me, you may be right!'

Her cheeks glowing now like two hot coals, she directed him the short distance to Ginny's home. Ginny lived closer to the village in a large modern bungalow. Several cars were already on the drive as Max pulled up.

'Looks as if everyone's here already,' Max commented.

Thea groaned. 'Oh no, that's Henry's car.' She nodded in the direction of a small red sports car parked at the top of the drive.

He paused as he opened the car door. 'And he is?'

She pulled a face as she climbed out. 'You remember the estate agent I told you about, the one who wants me to sell Stony Gables? That's Henry. We were at school together.'

Max closed the car door and clicked the fob to lock it. 'I take it you don't like him very much.'

Thea sighed. 'Henry's all right, I suppose. He just manages to annoy me every time we meet, and he's a bit too handy with his hands, if you know what I mean.'

Max gave a low rumble of laughter. 'Henry the octopus!'

Thea grinned. 'You've got it. He's been finding new premises for Laurence though, so that's why Ginny's invited him.'

Thea accepted Max's arm again and he escorted her up the drive to the front door. Her heart was racing as she rang the doorbell, but Max appeared perfectly calm and relaxed.

'Thea, Max — come in.' Ginny's husband, Laurence, swept them inside, shaking hands with Max and kissing Thea on the cheek.

'Tom's waiting in his bedroom for you, Thea. He wants you to pop in and see him before he goes to sleep,'

Laurence whispered in her ear as he relieved her of her thin shawl.

'I'd better not disappoint him then.' She smiled at Max and slipped away upstairs to Tom's room.

Tom was lying in bed doing a very unconvincing impression of being fast asleep.

'I thought you weren't coming,' he grumbled sleepily. Then, sitting upright, he added, 'You look nice. Like a sort of fairy with no wings.'

Thea laughed and ruffled his spiky hair. 'I suppose that's a compliment. Anyway, it's time you went to sleep.'

Scowling, he slid back down under the covers. 'Will you tuck me in, Thea?'

Smiling, she bent down and pulled the quilt up for him, then bent further to retrieve Action Man from the floor. She would love a little boy like Tom. Moments like these made her realise just how much. Maybe if things had worked out differently in her life when her father had first become ill . . .

'Thanks, Thea.' Tom snuggled down

under his covers.

'Night, Tom.' She closed the door behind her and made her way back downstairs to the conservatory, which ran along the back of the house. Ginny was waiting for her, a glass of white wine in her hand.

'Thanks for doing that, Thea. Hopefully he'll go off to sleep now. Here, I poured you a drink. I think you know everyone here.'

Thea accepted the glass and took a sip before looking around the room. 'Yes, I think so.'

'I had to ask Henry — sorry.' Ginny looked suitably apologetic. 'At least you've got Max with you so hopefully he'll leave you alone.'

As if drawn by a magnet, Thea looked back across the room and straight into Max's dark brown eyes. The corner of his mouth quirked upwards and he raised his glass slightly in her direction. Blushing, she turned away.

Ginny disappeared back into the

kitchen muttering something about soup and her place was rapidly filled by an all-too-familiar figure.

'Now where have you been hiding? I've been looking out for you.'

'Hello, Henry.' Thea took a pace back. Henry always managed to stand a little bit too close for comfort.

'I've still got people interested in that house of yours when you see sense and decide to sell.' He nudged her arm playfully with his elbow and moved a little nearer. Thea began to glance around for an escape route.

'There you are, darling. Ginny said to tell you supper's ready.' Max claimed her glass from her shaking hand and slipped his arm possessively around her waist. 'Shall we go through?'

Leaving Henry open-mouthed, Thea allowed Max to steer her away and into the dining-room.

'You looked as if you needed rescuing.' Max's low voice tickled her ear, and she was suddenly very aware of the lean strength of him beside her.

'Was it so obvious?'

She felt rather than saw him smile. 'Probably just to me.'

Flustered, she sat down and shook out her napkin, vaguely aware of the rest of Ginny's guests filing in for dinner.

Max took the seat opposite her, his handsome face intense in the flickering candlelight of the dinner table. Dragging her gaze away from his, she noticed Henry was seated farther down the table between the vicar and the chairwoman of the parish council. His round face had a distinctly put-out appearance and he directed a malevolent glare in Max's direction.

The evening was beginning to take on a surreal note where Thea was concerned, as her world seemed to shrink until all it held was the handsome man sitting opposite her.

★ ★ ★

Max was finding it difficult to concentrate on the dinner party conversation.

For some reason all his senses appeared to be attuned to Thea in her flirty diaphanous dress. Several times Laurence had to repeat something he had said and Ginny was giving him distinctly curious looks.

It came as a relief when the meal finally ended and Ginny invited them all back out into the conservatory for coffee and brandy. Before he could follow Thea, Ginny buttonholed him and drew him discreetly to one side.

'Is something going on between you and Thea?' She had a look on her face that Max knew only too well, the one that told him resistance was futile.

He held his hands up in a gesture of self-defence. 'Nothing, I swear. We've only just met.' His conscience gave a guilty twinge.

Ginny didn't look convinced. 'Mmm.'

'Thea's a very attractive girl.' He could feel embarrassment creeping like a tide around his collar.

'Yes, and she's not the kind of girl you usually go for. She's not the kind you can love and leave — she's a forever girl. Marriage, family, the works. So unless you've changed your spots, don't mess her about, Max.' A worried frown was creasing Ginny's forehead. 'She won't thank me for saying so, but she's had her fair share of heartaches these past few years.'

'I hear you, mother hen. I'll be good.' He kissed her cheek and went out into the conservatory, wondering what Ginny would have thought if she had heard the conversation he'd had with Thea that afternoon.

His eyes automatically sought out Thea's slim figure. She was engrossed in conversation with Laurence and the parish council chairwoman, whose name he had completely forgotten. Perhaps the warning from Ginny had come at the right time; it *would* be easy to become involved with Thea.

Max chatted amiably to the vicar and his wife for a while before noticing that Henry had worked his way around the guests and had managed to trap Thea by the door which led out to the garden. From the flushed expression on Henry's face and the way he was swaying slightly on his heels, Max guessed he had drunk more of the wine at dinner than was good for him.

Picking up Thea's shawl, Max edged away from his companions to draw closer to her.

'It's very kind of you to take an interest, Henry, but I really don't want to sell Stony Gables, especially not to some property developer.' He could hear Thea's voice now above the music and the chatter.

'The offer's there, remember. And if you're nice to old Henry I'm sure I can get you a great sale.' He leaned in over Thea and stroked the bare flesh at the top of her arm.

Max gritted his teeth and clenched his fist around the silky fabric of the shawl.

'I'm not selling, Henry.' Pointedly Thea lifted Henry's hand away from her arm.

'Perhaps you'll rethink when you start getting all the bills for the repair work that mausoleum needs,' Henry sneered.

Max moved closer so Thea could see him, and her eyes met his in an unspoken plea for help.

'Max, darling, is it time to go already?'

As Henry turned to see him approaching, Thea sidled away to slip her arm around Max's waist. A leap of electricity ran up Max's spine as Thea leaned into him, her soft curves moulding to his body in a perfect fit.

'Goodnight, Henry,' she added sweetly.

Max gave a curt nod in Henry's direction and draped the shawl over Thea's shoulders.

'We'd better say goodbye to Ginny, darling.' Her sparkling blue eyes, wickedly innocent, gleamed up at him, and Max wondered if she had any idea of how gorgeous she was.

Within a few minutes they had said their goodbyes and were escaping out of the front door into the cool air of the summer night.

'Phew! What a relief! Thanks, Max. Henry gets worse every time I see him.' Thea turned to smile at him, the pale skin of her arms gleaming in the moonlight, but her smile vanished when she looked at his face. 'I'm sorry, I guess that was pretty two-faced of me after what I said to you about deceiving Julia this afternoon.'

They crunched across the gravel to the car, the lights flashing as Max unlocked the doors. Climbing into her seat, Thea asked, 'Will it really make much difference to your sister if you tell her we're not engaged?'

Max slid the key into the ignition and glanced across at her. Her pretty face was screwed up in concern and she was twisting a loose tendril of her hair absently around her fingers.

'I don't know. Julia's very emotional at the moment and she sounded so much happier when she thought I was in a committed relationship. How she'll take it when I tell her the truth, I just don't know.'

'I see.'

Thea was silent for the short drive back to Stony Gables. Then, as Max swung the car on to the drive at the front of the house, she announced, 'All right, I'll do it!' with the air of a woman who had made a momentous decision.

Max stared at her with a bemused expression on his face. 'What are you going to do?'

'Help you out, of course! I'll do it — I'll be your pretend fiancée.' She turned in her seat to look him in the face, enthusiasm for the idea bubbling up inside her. 'I'll pretend to be engaged to you so you can persuade Julia to let Emily stay here,' she explained.

Max cut the car engine. 'I thought you said it would be a deceitful, wild idea that would never work.' He didn't sound keen.

She broke off eye contact and fiddled nervously with the thin silver strand of her bracelet. 'I've been thinking about it and I changed my mind.'

She had expected him to be delighted but, judging by the silence that met her last remark, he appeared to have had second thoughts about the plan. The excitement drained out of her as quickly as it had fizzed up. Great — now she looked like a fool, as usual.

'I know how much you care for Emily,' she began, trying to explain, 'and when I said goodnight to Tom earlier it made me realise how I would feel if she were my niece. I would want to do anything I could if I were in your shoes.'

Tucking Tom into bed had also reminded her of the feelings she'd had when her own plans for the future had crumbled during her father's illness. Plans which had included a fiancé and a wedding and a family.

Max sighed and unclipped his seat-belt. 'I don't know, Thea, I can't see how it could work. We hardly know one another. It was stupid of me to even suggest the idea.'

'It worked on Henry,' she protested, knowing in her heart that convincing a drunken man at a dinner party was hardly the same as fooling Max's sister.

Max's mouth curved into a lopsided smile. 'I think we just confused him.'

'I suppose you're right.' She felt unexpectedly deflated by his rejection of her offer. For a few wild moments she had really believed they could carry it off. She had even started to feel excited about it.

'I appreciate the offer, though.' Max gave her hand a gentle squeeze, sending a shiver through her body.

Hastily she pulled away and opened the car door. What was the matter with her tonight? Two glasses of wine and she was throwing herself at a stranger. Perhaps some fresh air would help her regain some perspective.

The stone gargoyles either side of the front door were silhouetted in the moonlight as she fumbled in her bag for the door key. She could smell the perfume from the yellow climbing roses her father had planted years ago as a present for her mother; the rain of the morning had intensified the strength of their scent in the warm night air.

She eventually managed to extricate the key and undo the lock.

'Would you like a coffee?' she asked as she opened the door.

'That would be nice, thanks.' He followed her down the hall to the kitchen, only pausing to pick up her shawl as it slid from her shoulders to the floor.

The kitchen light was dazzling after the darkness of the hallway. Thea dumped her bag on the table and switched on the kettle. Max carefully folded her shawl and placed it next to her bag.

She busied herself with finding the mugs and opening the coffee tin, her hand shaking a little as she spooned it into the mugs. Max crossed to the fridge and passed her the milk, his fingers brushing briefly against hers.

Her heart gave a leap at the contact and a warm wash of colour crept into her cheeks.

'What time will Julia and Emily arrive tomorrow?' She was pleased that her voice sounded steady, even if her hands weren't.

'Providing Julia doesn't get lost, probably around eleven.' Max cradled his mug in large capable hands, his dark eyes focused on the contents.

Thea took a sip of her coffee. 'I expect she's anxious to get everything settled and reassure herself about leaving Emily here.' She looked at Max. He was standing, as she herself so often did, leaning with his back against the warm rail of the Aga. 'I'm sure everything will work out.'

He smiled bleakly. 'I hope you're right. I'd hate Emily to have the kind of childhood Julia and I had. That's why making this arrangement work is so important.'

A pang of sympathy went through her at the sadness behind his words.

She felt certain this was the key to why he had declared himself so opposed to marriage. Seeing his sister's marriage hit problems would probably have reinforced his views, as well as sending his protective instinct into overdrive.

Thoughtfully she took another sip of her coffee and shoved the warning voice in her head back into its closet.

'Max is a very private person, Thea. Don't go trying your psychoanalysis stuff on him. Believe me, it won't work,' Ginny had warned her.

'I suppose I was lucky. I guess I had the kind of childhood most people would dream of.' She peeped at him from beneath her lashes to see what kind of effect her words had, hoping to find some clues to how his mind worked. 'I really hope I'll meet someone special one day and have a family of my own.'

Immediately she wished she could take the words back. Had he picked up on the wistful note in her voice? If he had, then she had just given a great impression of a sad old spinster desperate to land a man.

Max snorted derisively. 'I've seen too many marriages go wrong to fall for that happy-ever-after rubbish. Most relationships start to fail even before all the wedding cake has been eaten.'

She stared at him incredulously. How could anyone be that cynical!

'What about all the good relationships, all the people who celebrate their golden wedding anniversaries?'

He shook his head and swallowed the rest of his coffee. 'When you think of all the weddings that take place, most don't make five years, let alone fifty.'

'But what about love and romance?'

No wonder he had said there wouldn't be a Mrs Richardson. OK, so her own romances hadn't worked out up to now, but that didn't mean she had given up hope, although, to be honest, for a while it had been a close run thing.

'It's maybe all right for fairy tales,

but not for real life,' he said dismissively.

'Well, I think you're wrong. If you carry on thinking like that you're going to find yourself a lonely old man one day.'

She drank the rest of her coffee and placed her cup on the draining board. Contrarily, she didn't want to continue the conversation any more. But you started it, her conscience muttered rebelliously.

Max wished he hadn't stated his views so harshly when he saw the look in her eyes. From the horrified expression on her face, he might as well have declared himself a mass murderer.

What are you so concerned about anyway? his conscience jibed. You were only telling the truth; you were becoming much too attracted to her anyway. Ginny warned you, Thea isn't like Gabby and the other women you've dated.

'I guess our wedding's off then?' he tried to joke, hoping to coax a smile in place of the frown on her pretty face.

Thea shook her head gently, her deep blue eyes grave. 'I'm turning in. We've a busy day tomorrow. Goodnight, Max.'

He listened as she walked up the stairs.

'Well, you messed that up nicely!' he announced to the empty kitchen, before switching out the light to follow Thea up the stairs.

Fooling Julia

Waking the next morning, it took Max a few minutes to remember why he couldn't hear any traffic noise and why the room was bathed in a watery pale blue light. Memories of where he was and what he was doing there came flooding back, and he sank back against the pillows with a groan.

Glancing at his watch which he had propped up on the oak chest next to his bed, he realised it was still early. He listened for a moment, trying to work out what had disturbed him. Then he heard the noise again, somewhere nearby. A cockerel? Tom had said something about chickens.

The rest of the house was silent; Thea must not be an early riser.

He gazed around the room, wincing at the décor. It was no good; he was too restless to go back to sleep. Climbing out of bed, he pulled on his joggers and decided to go for a run.

★   ★   ★

Thea made a determined grab for Fred the cockerel's legs as he made a bid for freedom.

'Got you! Stupid bird, what do you have to make all that noise for? Anyone would think I was murdering you instead of collecting the eggs and cleaning your bedroom.'

She popped him back inside the run and secured the gate. Fred surveyed her sulkily from the hen-house roof and Thea pulled a face at him.

Usually she left it until a little later to let Fred and his three girlfriends out to play, but she was anxious to get all her mucky chores done early.

She didn't think she could face another humiliation like Max's arrival yesterday so today she was determined: she would be poised, welcoming, the perfect hostess. Absentmindedly she pulled a piece of straw from her hair. Who was she trying to kid? She had never been poised.

She wondered what Julia would be like, and little Emily. Poor child, Max was right about warring parents being tough on children. Thea had seen enough of the results in her classroom.

She hoped Fred hadn't disturbed Max. Leaning on the wire mesh fencing of the chicken run, she stared dreamily at the hens. Max seemed such a nice guy; it was a shame he had such fixed ideas about relationships. In his own way, he needed help as much as Emily and Julia did.

'You're up early.'

Surprised, she shot round to discover Max watching her from by the large oak tree. It looked as though he had been out running: his T-shirt was stained with sweat and he was panting slightly.

'You startled me!' she protested mildly.

'I'm sorry. You looked miles away.'

Even sweaty and rumpled he looked

good, while she must resemble a scarecrow, judging by the amount of straw that was sticking to her T-shirt and jeans.

'I was getting some of my jobs done early. Did Fred wake you up?'

He grinned. 'If Fred is the cockerel then yes, he did. It's fine though — gave me a chance to go for a run.'

'I suppose Stony Gables must be very different from where you live.'

'True. There aren't too many chickens in the centre of London — not live ones anyway.' He smiled at her.

'Breakfast will be ready in about an hour if that's OK. I have to finish off here and take a shower first.'

How did he always manage to catch her when she was looking her worst?

'Sounds great. I need a shower myself.' He jogged off back towards the house as Thea reached for her broom to tidy up the area outside the chicken run.

★ ★ ★

An hour and a half later, she had finished her messy chores, showered and changed. It had been difficult deciding what to wear. She didn't want Julia to think she was trying too hard or for Emily to feel nervous around her. At the same time she wanted to look smart, like the kind of woman you'd feel happy to leave your child with.

Eventually she had decided on navy trousers and a pretty white shirt with frills on the front. Her hair, as usual, had proved its untameable self, so she had pulled it back from her face and plaited it. Looking at her reflection in the mirror, she thought it made her look about twelve years old. Still, at least it was neat and tidy.

Max appeared to approve of her nursery teacher look when he came downstairs for breakfast.

'You look nice.' He sat down opposite her at the kitchen table and poured himself some coffee from the pot. Unused to compliments, Thea felt the colour creep into her cheeks at the warmth in his eyes.

'Thanks. So what's the plan?' she asked, buttering a slice of toast and taking a bite.

Max looked puzzled. 'Plan?'

'The one for when your sister arrives. You have to tell her we're not engaged or even a couple and at the same time convince her to leave Emily with you. I think that calls for a plan.'

He sighed and ran his fingers through his hair. 'Oh, *that* plan! I hoped I'd think of something this morning while I was out running.'

'And?'

He groaned. 'Nothing. Not even a glimmer of inspiration.' He glanced hopefully at her. 'How about you?'

'Well . . . ' She looked at him over the top of her coffee mug. 'Maybe we don't have to tell her we're not engaged.' She held up her hand to stop him before he could interrupt. 'I mean, unless she actually asks us, we could just say nothing.'

He stared at her for a moment. 'Lie

by omission, you mean?'

'No. Well, yes. Well, sort of. If she asks, we come clean, but by then hopefully Emily will be settling in and Julia can be persuaded that this is the best place for her to stay.'

'You really think that's a plan?' he asked incredulously.

'Do you have anything better?' She took another bite of her toast and waited for his response.

'Actually, no. I don't.' He grimaced and stirred his coffee.

'Well, I guess that means we wing it then,' she declared.

He looked at her for a long moment. 'This is never going to work.'

Thea shrugged. 'Neither of us can think of anything better and we both said we don't deliberately want to lie to Julia, so what else can we do?'

'OK, I agree. We'll just wait till she gets here and then see how everything goes.'

Thea lifted her mug and chinked it against his. 'To Operation Emily.'

The morning dragged by, even though Thea kept busy polishing, hoovering and baking, while listening out all the time for Julia's car. Max had disappeared into the study to work on his laptop, but the tense expression on his face when she took him a cup of tea told her he was as nervous as she was.

When the sound of a car pulling up on the drive finally made itself heard, Thea nearly missed it. She ran back downstairs just as Max skidded into the hall, his dark eyes anxious as his gaze met hers. Taking a deep breath to steady her nerves, she continued more slowly down the last few stairs and opened the front door with Max at her side.

A young woman was emerging from an expensive four-wheel-drive car. Opening the rear door, she lifted down a small child. Max strode across the gravel to greet them, Thea following at a slight distance, a shiver of apprehension running down her spine.

Julia was dark-haired like Max, but she was as small and slender as he was tall and muscular. She looked fragile, as if a gust of wind would blow her away. Her eyes, also brown like her brother's, were shadowed and lined from stress.

Max had swept Emily up into his arms and the child clung to his neck as if her life depended on it, her small face revealing a mix of excitement and fear.

Julia gave Thea a wan smile as she approached. 'You must be Thea. I've been looking forward to meeting you ever since Max finally had the decency to tell me about you.'

'It's nice to meet you, too. And Emily.'

The little girl was staring at her with huge, solemn eyes, and Thea felt her heart going out to her; she looked so small and scared. Max's soundless plea for help rang as clearly in Thea's mind as if he had voiced it out loud.

'Come into the house and I'll make you a cup of tea. I expect Emily would like a drink of juice.'

Thea led the way towards the house, asking Julia questions about her journey as they made their way into the hall.

'A bear!'

Thea turned. Emily was still clinging to Max's neck, her eyes wide with astonishment as she looked at the stuffed grizzly in his Panama hat.

'He looks funny,' the child decided.

'This is Mr Smith,' Thea introduced him and encouraged Emily to shake his paw. 'He's a very polite bear.'

Emily giggled. 'I like him.'

Thea was surprised to see Julia wiping away a tear from the corner of her eyes.

'I haven't heard her laugh for weeks,' she whispered, her pale face distraught. Impulsively Thea gave her hand a reassuring squeeze as she took them through into the kitchen.

Max carried Emily to the window to show her the view of the garden and to tell her about the little pony that lived in the neighbouring field. Thea could feel Julia's eyes burning into her back as she filled the kettle and set it on the hob to boil.

'You're very different from how I imagined you,' Julia said.

'Oh?' Feeling a little guilty, Thea poured Emily some apple juice and opened the biscuit tin.

'I thought you'd be more like Gabby and some of the other women Max has dated. To be honest, I was really nervous about meeting you.'

Max didn't seem to have heard his sister's comments as he set Emily down and came over to join them.

Turning to fill the teapot with the boiling water, Thea wondered about the kind of women Max dated. From things Ginny had told her in the past, he liked sophisticated, elegant and un-demanding women.

Blushing at the way her thoughts were leading her, she tucked some escaping strands of her hair behind her ears and concentrated on making the tea.

'How did you two meet?' Julia wanted to know.

'Ginny introduced us.' Thea crossed her fingers behind her back, though it wasn't a lie, she just wasn't admitting that that had only been yesterday.

Julia glanced at Thea and then at Max, a slightly puzzled expression on her face. 'It must have been fairly recently.'

'Well, you know what they say, when you meet someone and everything just seems right . . . ' Max chipped in.

'I can honestly say I think I made quite an impression on our first meeting,' Thea said, causing Max to choke on his cup of tea, though he managed to turn it into a cough.

'When can I see the tower? Uncle Max said I've got a princess's bedroom.' Emily plonked her empty glass back on the table and wiped her mouth with the back of her hand.

'Well, why doesn't Uncle Max take you to see your room while Mummy finishes her tea?' Thea suggested.

'Great idea. Come on, pest, let's go and explore.' Max led Emily out of the kitchen, leaving the two women alone.

'I was so pleased when Max told me the news and now I've met you I feel much happier about Emily staying with you both. I can see you're a natural with children.'

Guilt settled on Thea's shoulders like a heavy cloak.

Julia looked at her shyly. 'I hope you didn't mind me mentioning Gabby's name. Paul, my husband, is always telling me I'm tactless.'

'It's OK, Max told me about her.' Thea shuffled her feet nervously under the table. Who was Gabby? This was going to be harder to pull off than she had first thought.

'I'm glad he's met you,' Julia was saying. 'I think you're just the kind of person Max needs in his life.'

In spite of her guilty conscience, Thea was intrigued, but before Julia could say anything else Emily came bursting back into the kitchen to seize her mother's hand. 'Mummy, come and see, come and see!'

While Julia allowed her daughter to lead her out of the kitchen, Thea placed the empty mugs on the draining board.

'Thank you for doing this.' Max's voice was suddenly very close to her ear. She hadn't heard him come back in. 'It's the first time in weeks that I've seen Emily look happy.'

A crackle of electricity shot through her bones at his proximity as she turned to face him.

'Julia seems like a really nice person,' she said, though all she could think of was how close Max's lips were to hers.

'She's not bad, for a kid sister,' he murmured, as his lips met hers.

A charge of sensations fizzed around her body and her knees were like cotton wool. Unbidden, her arms slid around his neck, her fingers caressing the hair at the nape of his neck.

'Whoops, sorry! I didn't mean to interrupt!'

They sprang apart at the sound of

Julia's voice from the doorway and Thea turned to see Max's sister and his little niece watching them with bright-eyed curiosity.

Heat flooded through her. Of all the embarrassing situations to be caught in. She was sure from the stunned expression on Max's face when he saw his sister standing in the doorway that kissing her had definitely not been a part of some premeditated scheme to convince Julia that the engagement was for real. Even more cringeworthy was the way she had been kissing him back. He would think she was a desperate spinster out to hook a husband.

Boy, could he kiss, though! She couldn't remember feeling like this before, even when Jon had kissed her — and she had planned to marry him.

Meanwhile Max was groaning inwardly, hoping Thea wouldn't think he had timed his kiss deliberately, although he was a little hazy about who had been kissing who.

Thea tugged nervously on one of her

earrings as she edged towards the door, her face pink with embarrassment.

'I'll, erm . . . I, er, just have to go and check on something.' She made her escape through the back door into the garden.

* * *

'I'm sorry,' Julia said. 'I didn't mean to embarrass you both.' For the first time in ages her eyes were bright and alert, her eager expression more like the old Julia, before all her problems with Paul had begun. Max hoped it was a good sign.

'That's OK,' he said. 'What do you think? Do you like it here?'

Julia laughed. 'Do you mean do I like it *here*? Or is that your way of asking if I like Thea?'

'*I* like it here, Uncle Max. I like my bedroom and the toys.' Emily's dark eyes were serious as she emerged from her mother's side, clutching a battered old rag-doll.

Julia looked lovingly at her small

daughter. 'Would you like to stay here with Uncle Max and Thea instead of going to Auntie Nettie's house?'

Emily nodded and cuddled the doll close to her. 'I like being with Uncle Max and Thea's pretty.'

Max exhaled in silent relief; a degree of deception had to be worthwhile if it meant Emily was happy.

'Well, we'll see. And for what it's worth, big brother, I do like Thea. I like her very much.' Julia was smiling and Max hoped the spectre of Aunt Nettie was receding.

'Thea wears rings on her toes,' Emily pointed out, her lips pursed as if she wasn't sure whether that was a good thing or not.

'Did you find the big box of old jewellery she put in your room?' Max steered the subject away from Thea's dress sense. Julia's need for their mother's approval as a child had stifled most of her creativity and led to a legacy of a need for order and convention.

Emily nodded enthusiastically. 'And there's a whole pile of dressing-up things.'

'Thea certainly knows how to appeal to a little girl's heart,' Julia observed. 'She'll be a great mother when you two start your own family.'

Max's conscience kicked in response to the image that popped into his mind of Thea with a child on her lap. A child with dark brown eyes — a child of his.

'We'd better bring the bags in from the car,' Julia suggested.

'I'll bring them in for you.'

Max followed them outside, his mind still whirling from the thought of Thea as the mother of his children.

* * *

He had a very curious expression on his face, Thea observed, when he rejoined her in the kitchen as she prepared lunch for them all.

'How do you think it's going?' she asked as she drained the potatoes at the sink.

'Emily really likes it here.' His voice sounded cautious.

'Well, that's good, isn't it?'

'Julia still thinks we're engaged, and I don't think we can risk telling her the truth now. She'd never trust me again, let alone leave Emily here.'

'I suppose finding you kissing me probably didn't help.'

'*You* kissed *me!*' Max sounded indignant.

'I seem to remember *you* started it!' Cheek, trying to blame her!

Her cheeks grew warmer as she recalled him pulling her close, his strong arms encircling her body . . . and her instinctive response to his touch.

'Well, whatever, the damage is done now,' he pointed out.

'You always propose in the most romantic ways,' Thea commented as she bustled past him and began setting the table, but as the humour in the situation suddenly struck her it was all she could do to stop her lips twitching with laughter. Poor Max looked so flustered. Did he think she was expecting him to honour the engagement in some way?

He glared at her. 'Thea, this isn't funny.'

Immediately she sobered. 'No, it's not, but I don't see that we have much choice except to continue pretending.'

He fingered the corner of a linen napkin. 'And if we're going to carry on with this, then we have to make it more convincing.' He avoided her gaze.

Thea stared at him. 'What do you mean?'

'We'll have to act more like a couple. You know . . . ' He glanced unhappily at her. 'Holding hands, kissing — '

Thea felt as if he had thrown a bucket of cold water over her. He obviously hadn't enjoyed kissing her. The look on his face and the tone of his voice suggested he couldn't think of anything that could possibly be more unpleasant than holding hands and kissing.

'I see.' She knew the tone of her voice

was cold enough to make the iceberg that sank the Titanic seem positively cosy, but Max didn't appear to notice.

'It's only while Julia's here. She's anxious to get Emily settled so she can join Paul in Singapore. It shouldn't be too hard.'

She wasn't sure if he was talking to her or to himself. Indignation crackled down her spine and she banged the last plate down on the table.

'Well, while you steel yourself for the task ahead I'll go and sound the gong for dinner.' She whisked off into the hall and vented her feelings on the dinner gong at the foot of the stairs.

★ ★ ★

Fortunately Julia and Emily kept the conversation flowing during lunch, while Max was overly solicitous, offering her the salt and passing her the wine.

'When are you going to show me your ring, Thea? You have such pretty taste in jewellery I expect it's really lovely.' Julia looked pointedly at the bare space on Thea's engagement finger.

'Ring?' Thea stared blankly till a kick on her ankle from Max jogged her brain back into gear. 'Oh, my engagement ring? Well, I haven't actually got one yet. We did look at some but it's so hard to choose.' She scrabbled around in her mind for an excuse and hoped Julia couldn't tell she was lying. 'We haven't had much time really and, well, you know . . . ' She petered out lamely.

Julia looked horrified. 'Max, you must get her a ring! Tell you what, why don't you two go into town this afternoon and have a good look round while I help Emily unpack and settle in?'

'Oh, but we couldn't! I'd feel like such a bad hostess.' Thea looked meaningfully at Max, willing him to think of a good reason why they shouldn't follow Julia's suggestion. She couldn't possibly let him buy her a ring.

It was ridiculous!

'If you're sure you and Emily will be all right here on your own this afternoon, then I think that's a great idea,' he replied smoothly.

Thea couldn't believe her ears. She had expected Max to back her up, not to go along with the idea! What was he playing at?

'We'll go straight after lunch then, darling, shall we?' he said, topping up Thea's wine glass. His dark eyes warned her against protesting too much.

'Can't wait,' she said through gritted teeth, and raised her glass in a tiny salute which went unobserved by Julia and Emily.

'You could get a ring like this one. It's really pretty.' Emily proudly showed off a huge plastic ring with a clear stone in the top. 'If you press it, it flashes. Look.' She demonstrated the ring's magical ability to flash green and red.

'I think that's lovely, Emily. I can only hope that there'll be another one like it in the shop,' Thea remarked, thinking a ring like Emily's would probably be entirely appropriate for this fake engagement.

As soon as dessert was finished, Julia leapt to her feet and began to clear the dishes.

'You two go. I'll do these.' She waved away Thea's protests. 'I'll enjoy spending time with Emily and helping her settle. Besides, it's important to get a ring. It makes things more official, and then later on, when you get back, we can plan the party.'

'Party?' Max echoed, hardly daring to look at Thea.

'To celebrate your engagement, silly!' Julia tutted as she carried the dishes over to the sink.

'Do we need a party?' Max intercepted her as she returned to the table to collect another load of dishes.

'Well, you have to do something to celebrate. It's not every day you get engaged. And to be honest, brother dear, I didn't think you would *ever* settle down and commit to one woman.'

Julia swept past, leaving Max floundering in her wake.

'I don't know if Thea and I want a party. We were planning on keeping everything very low-key.'

Julia raised her eyebrows. 'Low-key? I'm sure Thea will want to meet all your friends and colleagues. I bet you haven't had a chance to introduce her to everyone yet.'

'Well, no, but — '

'Then a party will be perfect. Thea can meet everyone at the same time.'

Thea looked as dazed as Max felt, and he rallied again.

'Julia, I'm not sure about this. Wouldn't it be better to wait a while?' He tried to think of a fool-proof excuse to dissuade her. The problem was, once his sister got an idea in her head she was very difficult to sway.

'What for?' Julia stared at him, her eyes round with astonishment.

'Look, we'll discuss this later when

we come back from town.'

Julia looked disappointed and Thea attempted to console her. 'It's a lovely idea, Julia, and very kind of you. Max and I will think about it while we're out, I promise.'

Julia shrugged and continued to clear the table but Max could tell that she was put-out by his lack of enthusiasm.

★　★　★

Thea was unusually quiet as they got into Max's car to drive to town, a frown puckering her forehead.

'I'm sorry about the party idea. I'd forgotten about Julia's passion for observing all the social niceties,' he said as he started the car engine.

'I suppose if we'd thought this through properly we should have expected something like this.'

Glancing at her, he noticed she was twiddling her long silver earring absently between her fingers. She always played with her jewellery when she had something on her mind.

'Where's the best jeweller's shop?' They were already at the outskirts of the small market town nearest to Thea's village.

'There's only one. It's near the church, not far from Henry's estate agency.' She directed him to the car park at the back of the church.

As he parked the car and switched off the engine, she turned towards him. 'Max, we don't have to buy a proper ring. It seems so silly when Julia will be gone in a couple of days.' The worried frown was still creasing her forehead.

'And what will she think if we go back and you have something that looks like it came out of a cracker?' he asked.

'That I have bad taste?' she suggested feebly.

He shook his head. 'If it makes you feel any better, I'm sure I'll be able to sell it afterwards if you don't want to keep it. As far as I'm concerned, it's a small price to pay to make Emily happy.'

The jeweller congratulated them both profusely when they asked to see the selection of engagement rings. Standing by the glass-topped counter while he unlocked the display cabinets, Thea wondered wistfully what it would be like to be standing there with a man she loved for real, to be choosing a ring she would wear with pride and pleasure for the rest of her life, like she had thought before when she was with Jon . . .

The jeweller placed the burgundy velvet pads and their glittering contents on the counter with a reverent air and Thea forced herself to concentrate on the task in hand. Ordinarily she loved to buy jewellery. Some women loved shoes but Thea's addiction, when she had any money, was silver and gold.

'Do you like any of these?' Max had already rejected two trays as being too cheap.

Thea hesitated. She felt guilty that Max was being coerced into buying her a ring. She knew his views on marriage, so this must be a real nuisance for him.

'That sapphire one is quite nice.' she indicated a small sapphire ring with a diamond surround, but Max threw her a shrewd glance and she knew he wasn't going to fall for her ploy of choosing one of the cheaper rings on the tray.

He unerringly selected the one she really coveted, a beautiful square-cut emerald which glistened alone on a fine platinum band.

'Try this one,' he said.

He slid the ring over her finger and they both admired it as it twinkled in the bright lights of the shop.

'Oh, Max, I couldn't.' The protest came out as a whisper as she watched the light reflecting off the clear green stone.

'We'll take this one,' Max said firmly, and the jeweller started to put away the other trays of rings. 'It's perfect and it's you, Thea.'

His dark eyes locked with hers and for a fleeting moment Thea forgot all about the jeweller smiling benevolently at them from behind the counter. She forgot all about the engagement not being real, all about Max not being really in love with her.

'Thank you,' she murmured.

His lips brushed hers and the world tilted on its axis.

'You're welcome.' His voice was husky and she turned away quickly as the jeweller cleared his throat and slid the ring's little box into a small bag.

The warm afternoon sunshine greeted them as they stepped outside on to the high street. Max slid the package into his jacket pocket. Thea was still turning the emerald on her finger, admiring it.

'It's beautiful. I still think it's a bit over the top, though, Max. The sapphire would have done just as well.'

He paused and took her hand in his to examine the ring, his warm capable fingers sliding around hers. 'No, it had to be this one. It looks beautiful on you.' His face had an odd expression, almost wistful.

A frisson of awareness moved along Thea's skin from where he was still holding her hand, and she swallowed hard.

'Emily will be disappointed that it doesn't flash,' she joked.

'She'll get over it.' He smiled gently and before Thea had realised what he intended, he raised her hand to his lips and kissed it gently.

'I guess this makes us official then,' she murmured. Her heart was hammering against her ribcage.

'I guess so.'

It was like being in a wonderful dream bubble. No one else on the busy high street existed except her and Max. He carried on holding her hand as they strolled along in the summer sunshine back towards the car.

'Max!'

The bubble popped and Thea looked round to see who had called his name. From the displeased look on Max's face, it was clearly someone he had no desire to see.

A tall, elegant woman sashayed towards them. 'Max, darling! I didn't expect to run in to you in this little town.' The woman swooped in and air-kissed both his cheeks, forcing him to relinquish his hold on Thea's hand.

'I could say the same for you, Gabby.'

Thea surveyed the woman narrowly. So this was Gabby, Max's ex-girlfriend. Her stomach plummeted, the girl was gorgeous, there was no other word for her. Her sleek dark hair looked as if it never had a fight with a hairbrush in its life. She had large dark eyes, flawless skin and a perfect figure. To Thea's surprise, as she stood looking at Gabby's beautiful clothes and shoes, she thought she had never disliked anyone so much in her life.

'I told you I was looking for a little weekend place in the country, silly!' Gabby purred.

'I don't believe you've met Thea.' Max slid his hand back into Thea's and gave her a warning squeeze. 'Thea, this is Gabby. Gabby, this is Thea, my fiancée.'

Thea watched the play of emotions on Gabby's beautiful face. The woman couldn't have looked any more stunned if she had been slapped. It look her a full minute to assimilate what Max had just said, and Thea almost felt sorry for her.

'Well, congratulations.' Gabby dived on Thea's hand to look at the ring, as if she had to see it with her own eyes in order to believe it. She looked at Thea incredulously, and that look made Thea aware of every single fault in her appearance. The new trousers and pretty shirt she had thought so smart that morning suddenly seemed creased and tatty when viewed through the other woman's eyes.

Gabby turned her attention back to Max.

'I had no idea, this is such a surprise! Have you known each other long?'

Max was as expressionless as a poker player. 'Not really, but when you meet the right person, you just know.'

Gabby's eyes widened. 'You've certainly changed your tune,' she said suspiciously.

'Love does that,' Max murmured.

Thea couldn't stay silent any longer; sharp little spears of jealousy were prodding her into speech. 'Max, we have to go — Julia and Emily will be waiting for us. It was nice to meet you, Gabby.'

She hoped she didn't sound too insincere, and she very much doubted if Gabby had found it a pleasure to meet her. From the way her lip had curled on seeing Thea's clothes and her wayward hair, it was plain that she thought Max had gone stark raving mad.

'I expect we shall be meeting again soon. We're going to be neighbours,' Gabby announced, a triumphant gleam in her eyes when she noticed Thea's surprise.

'You've bought a house here?' Max sounded as surprised as Thea was. His jaw was set ominously, and although to a casual bystander he would have given the impression of a man having a pleasant chat, Thea knew him well enough by now to know it was a sign of real displeasure. She could feel the tension humming through his frame from the touch of his hand alone.

'Just renting for a little while. I like to get a feel of a place and with the weather so nice I thought I'd be able to make the most of the summer,' Gabby returned.

Max raised one eyebrow. 'I hope you like country life then, Gabby. You might find it a little quiet after the city.'

'Oh, I shall have some friends down from London, and give a few dinner parties. You and Tina will come, of course.' Gabby flashed them a self-satisfied smirk.

Thea knew Gabby had got her name wrong on purpose, but forced herself to paste on a smile, determined not to let the other woman get the upper hand.

'I wouldn't count on us.' She made a show of clinging to Max's hand and giggled coyly. 'Being newly engaged, we like to spend our time together. Alone, just the two of us. I'm sure you'll understand.'

Max's lips flickered upwards at the corners, amused. Thea suspected that it was a long time since anyone had called Gabby's bluff.

★ ★ ★

As they walked away, with Thea's slender hand still in his grasp, Max began to laugh. 'Well done!'

'You don't think I overdid it?' she asked as they rounded the corner of the church.

'No, you were great.'

'I wondered if I'd gone too far. But I got the impression that you weren't very pleased to see her.' This came out in a bit of a rush and he had to bend his head to catch what she said.

He shrugged. 'Gabby and I dated for a while, but it's like I told you — I'm not planning on getting married to anyone. I thought Gabby felt the same but then she started hinting about moving in and accepting long-term invitations for us as a couple, so we broke up.'

He sensed Thea was turning his reply over in her mind. Quite why he felt uncomfortable about that, he wasn't really sure, but somehow he did.

'She's very attractive.'

He glanced at her. 'Yes, she is.'

But Gabby was a clone of all the other women he had ever dated. Tall, slim and elegant with a wealthy background. Women who were discreet, enjoyed lunches and dinners out and a partner to escort them to the latest theatre or gallery opening.

He couldn't picture Gabby ever getting up at six o'clock to clean out a chicken run, and Gabby would never have got stuck in a window! He distinctly remembered mentioning to her his intention of caring for Emily while Julia was away. Her cold indifference to Emily's welfare had been the prompt he had been waiting for to end their shallow relationship.

They stopped beside the car. Thea still appeared to be deep in thought.

'How long do you think it'll take for word to get around?' Max asked as he unlocked the car door and Thea got in.

'What, about our engagement? Probably a couple of days, I suppose. Nothing's a secret for very long around here.' She froze, pulling across her seatbelt. 'Oh, no!'

'What's the matter?'

'What are we going to tell Ginny?' she wailed.

She had a point. Ginny was never going to swallow the story of their engagement being the real thing. What's more, if she spoke to Julia, which she inevitably would since they were good friends, they would be well and truly rumbled.

'We'll have to tell her the truth. That it's all pretend,' Thea decided.

Max was thinking quickly. 'We'll call at Ginny's house on the way home and try to get her and Laurence on side.'

Thea was nibbling on her lower lip, her blue eyes troubled. 'I hate having to ask them to lie.'

Max wasn't looking forward to it either. He guessed Ginny would have a lot to say on the subject, and most of it would be directed at him. He glanced at Thea as they drove towards Ginny's house, his eyes drawn to the emerald ring sparkling on her slender finger.

How had a simple misunderstanding mushroomed into all this? He sighed deeply, remembering the look on Thea's face when he had placed the ring on her finger. For a split second he had forgotten the engagement was fake and a sense of rightfulness about the situation had engulfed him, momentarily sweeping him away into Thea's romantic fantasyland.

He had to get a grip on himself. Marriage is for idiots, he reminded himself sternly. This pretend engagement was only for Emily's benefit. Once Julia and Paul had sorted out their marriage and Emily was settled, then he would be out of there. Back to London and the peace and quiet of his flat, back to his normal life.

Turning in to Ginny's driveway, he suppressed the thought that resuming his normal life suddenly seemed very unappealing.

More About Max

Any hopes Thea had been entertaining about Ginny being sympathetic to their plight appeared to evaporate as Max explained what had happened. Several times during the telling of the story, she glanced at Thea, and at Max, and then at the glittering emerald on Thea's finger, as if she couldn't believe what she was hearing. The worst of it was, Thea didn't blame her.

They were sitting in Ginny's sunny conservatory. The ceiling fan whirred gently overhead and a soft breeze blew in through the open French doors.

'What were you thinking?' Ginny finally demanded. 'I expect Thea to come up with hare-brained schemes like this, but *you*, Max!' She shook her head.

'We didn't plan this,' Thea protested. How come she was getting the blame anyway? It was mostly Max's fault. Emily was his niece, after all, and he had been the one to mislead Julia originally.

'Now *that* I *can* believe!' Ginny scoffed.

'Will you help us?' Max's dark eyes betrayed his anxiety.

Thea stroked the cool, comforting silver strand of her earring while she waited for Ginny to come to a decision.

'Ordinarily, I'd say you should come clean and tell Julia the truth, but . . . '

Thea waited with bated breath. They couldn't tell Julia, not now. It had all gone too far.

'But Max is right about Emily. I don't think it would be fair to upset her, and Julia's stressed enough already,' Ginny concluded.

'Oh, thanks, Ginny.' Thea leaned over and hugged her.

'That doesn't mean I approve,' Ginny warned, 'and I hope you'll get things straightened out as soon as everything settles down.'

'Well, Julia's leaving in a few days.

She wants to fly out and join Paul as soon as she's got Emily settled in,' Max told her.

Ginny considered this.

'And this party you mentioned, when is she thinking of holding that?' she wanted to know.

Max groaned and ran his hand despairingly through his hair. 'I hoped she might not have time before she leaves, but knowing Julia, she won't rest till she's organised something.'

'Maybe she'll settle for a dinner party instead?' Thea suggested. 'We could go to The Limes. You know the place, Ginny — that new bistro that's opened in town.' Thea sat up enthusiastically on her cane chair. Dinner would be much better than a party. She could cope with a dinner.

Max leaned forward in his seat, equally enthused. 'She might go for that. It would be easier to arrange at short notice.' He smiled approvingly at Thea and her heart gave a disconcerting leap.

Ginny looked at her watch. 'Tom and Laurence will be back from the park in a minute. I'll tell Laurence once Tom is out of earshot.'

'Good idea,' Thea agreed. 'I remember the last time Tom overheard something he shouldn't have.' She grinned at Ginny. 'Is Mrs Dawes talking to you yet?'

'That bad, huh?' Max shook his head and reached out a hand to pull Thea to her feet, sending a tingle through her skin. 'Come on, we'd better go. Julia and Emily will be waiting for us.'

Ginny followed them to the front door.

'Are you sure this is just a pretend engagement?' Ginny's whisper in Thea's ear as she was stepping out of the door made her turn round.

'I'm doing this for Emily,' Thea murmured as Max strode off down the drive.

Ginny frowned. 'I just don't want to see you get hurt. Don't fool yourself into thinking any of this is real. Max isn't the marrying kind.'

Thea felt a little stab of pain piercing her heart. 'I know. He told me.'

Max clicked the key fob to open the car door and waited for Thea to join him. He wondered what Ginny was saying to make her frown.

'Is everything all right?' he couldn't resist asking as they pulled out of the drive.

'Yes, fine.' Thea looked a little flushed and he had the uncomfortable feeling that Ginny had given her a warning of some kind.

Perhaps that was a good thing. Kissing Thea this morning had been far too pleasant. He felt as if he were on some crazy roller-coaster ride that he couldn't get off.

* ⋆ ⋆

Julia and Emily were in the garden when they arrived back at the house. Emily was on Thea's old garden swing, urging her mother to push her higher as

112

she whizzed back and forth, her small face glowing with pleasure.

Scenes like this made a little deception a low price to pay, Max thought, as he and Thea walked down the path towards them. Fun was something that had been missing from Emily's life for some time now.

'Watch me, Uncle Max!' Emily yelled. Julia, too, was smiling. Some of the tension which had been weighing her down so heavily on her arrival appeared to have lifted.

Julia looked eagerly at Thea's hand and Max quashed the tiny feeling of guilt which crept into his heart when he saw the joy on his sister's face as she congratulated Thea. It wasn't going to be as easy as he had first thought to end this pretend engagement when the time came.

'I'm so glad you found something you like. It's really beautiful. Now you've just got to have a party to show it off!'

Max met Thea's clear blue gaze and

cleared his throat. 'We talked about that, and there's not much time to organise things — '

'But you've got to have a party!' Julia interrupted.

'We thought maybe a dinner instead? It'll be much easier to arrange at short notice,' Thea said. 'There's a lovely new bistro opened in town. You could help me work out who to invite. It wouldn't be so much work and it'd still be fun. What do you think?'

Julia considered, then smiled happily. 'You're right. There isn't much time before I leave. That sounds like a great idea.'

'Can I go?' Emily had been listening to the conversation and her face lit up at the mention of the word 'party.'

'This will be a little late at night for you, sweetie,' Julia said.

Emily's face fell and Thea stepped in quickly to add, 'But I'll arrange a special party for you when Mummy has gone on her holiday.'

'Do I get a new dress?' Emily asked

hopefully, and her mother laughed.

'I suppose that's fair,' she said and lifted Emily from the swing.

'And will Daddy come?'

Julia hesitated for a moment before answering: 'I expect we'll both be back before you know it.'

Max looked at Thea, knowing she had picked up on the tiny quaver in Julia's voice.

'I think I know a little girl who's probably ready for her tea,' Thea said. 'How about Uncle Max giving you a piggy back up to the house to wash your hands while I go and make us some sandwiches?'

Emily beamed and ran over to Max, holding up her arms ready to be lifted on to his shoulders. Thea slipped her arm through Julia's and Max left them to follow behind as he raced up the path with Emily on his shoulders, making her squeal with pretend terror as he ran.

'Are you all right?' Concerned, Thea looked at Julia's pale face.

Julia sighed. 'I'm OK. I just hope that when Paul and I meet up we can sort ourselves out. We've said some terrible things to each other over the last few months and poor Emily has felt it more than either of us realised.'

She looked to be on the verge of tears and Thea felt torn as she heard Emily's innocent laughter ahead of them on the path.

'I'm sure you'll work things out,' Thea murmured in sympathy.

'I hope so, for Emily's sake, if not ours,' Julia returned.

Max raised a questioning eyebrow as they clattered in through the back door of the kitchen where he and Emily were washing their hands at the sink. Thea answered him with a barely perceptible nod as she filled the kettle ready to make tea.

Max took the hint and scooped Emily into his arms, to carry her giggling into the lounge with a promise to show her Thea's video collection.

Julia accepted the mug of tea Thea

offered her and stared sadly out of the window.

'I don't know what you must think of the family you're marrying into, Thea. I suppose Max has told you all about our childhood?'

'He told me a little,' Thea said guardedly.

'He always swore he was never going to get married or have children. He seems to have changed so much since he met you,' Julia mused.

Thea's conscience nipped her and heat flooded into her cheeks, but Julia sipped her tea, not noticing.

'That's why I didn't want to leave Emily with him,' Julia went on, 'even though when we were little Max always looked after me. He always sorted out my problems.' She turned to Thea, her eyes dark with anguish. 'But this is one problem I have to sort out for myself.'

Thea frowned. 'But Max loves Emily.' She didn't quite understand. She could see why Julia wanted to be independent, but there was still a piece missing from the jigsaw. There had to be more to Max's reluctance to commit.

Julia nodded. 'Yes, but I wasn't sure if he was up to handling the twenty-four-hour-a-day responsibility of caring for a child her age. Max had shut himself off from his emotions for such a long time, Thea. I wasn't sure if just spending a few hours with her every weekend was enough preparation.' She sighed. 'I shouldn't have worried; since he's met you the change in him is obvious.'

Thea blinked. She didn't think she was that good an actress, or Max that good an actor, for that matter.

'It's the way he looks at you all the time. And he's much less uptight when you're around.' Julia burbled on, oblivious to Thea's stunned silence. 'I can see he's mad about you.'

More like mad *at* me most of the time, Thea thought as she pulled the bread from the bread bin ready to start making sandwiches.

'Oh, by the way — ' Julia blushed.

' — I hope I'm not going to embarrass you here, but this morning when I was upstairs — ' She stopped and put her hands on Thea's arm. 'Well, I couldn't help noticing, and it's very sweet of you, but I'm a realist and I know what modern relationships are like.'

Thea stared at her, bewildered. 'I'm sorry?'

'What I'm trying to say is, you and Max needn't have separate bedrooms on my account. After all, you are practically married.'

Thea was so startled she nicked the end of her finger with the bread knife.

'I could see Max had moved into the blue bedroom in a hurry, so I moved his things right back into your room. I would feel awful if you two felt you had to be apart because of me.'

Thea sucked the end of her cut finger and looked incredulously at Julia. 'That's very kind of you, but really, we — er — we aren't — I mean — we were thinking of Emily,' she improvised desperately.

Her mind had gone into a panic. She was very traditional in her views on relationships and marriage, but would telling the truth somehow jeopardise Max's plan?

'Oh, it's all right. I told Emily you and her Uncle Max are getting married and you're going to be her aunty. She understands.' Thea frowned. It wasn't what she would have wanted to teach Emily about relationships, but she wasn't the child's mother — it wasn't up to her.

Tutting over the cut on Thea's finger, Julia added, 'Where do you keep your plasters?'

Julia rummaged in the dresser drawer where Thea had indicated, returned triumphantly with a dressing, and got to work on the cut.

'There, that's better. I'll give you a hand, and then after tea we can draw up a list for the dinner party and book the table.'

All the while she was cutting the bread and washing the salad, Thea kept trying to think of a way out of sharing her room with Max. When she had started letting rooms for bed and breakfast, she had taken one of the smaller bedrooms for herself. Which meant there was room for her double bed, a wardrobe and a small chest of drawers, but not much else.

★   ★   ★

Once tea was over and Julia had taken a tired Emily upstairs to bath her and put her to bed, Thea thought she had better break the news about the bedroom arrangements to Max.

'But she can't . . . She hasn't . . . ' Max looked as shell-shocked as Thea had been; a frown creased his forehead, the exasperation evident on his face.

'She can and she has. I've been trying to think of a way out of it, but I've drawn a blank. I could just tell her my views on that kind of thing, I suppose . . . ' But other than that she couldn't see any way of changing rooms without arousing Julia's suspicions. And since she would be gone in three days' time anyway, it hardly seemed worth rocking the boat. If it all helped to settle things for Emily . . .

'I'm so sorry, Thea. But don't worry — I'll sleep on the floor,' Max said desperately.

Thea laughed. 'In my room? You'd be lucky if we ever managed to straighten you out again if you tried that on the amount of floor space I've got!'

The sound of Julia's feet on the stairs brought the discussion to a halt. She had brought her notebook and flipped it open as she sat down on the settee.

'I thought if we work out roughly how many people you plan to invite, we could book the table.'

'I'll fetch us a drink,' Thea suggested. Max certainly felt as if he needed one. A large whisky would have been just the ticket but he hadn't noticed anything that strong in Thea's cupboards.

'By the way, I placed the announcement in The Times while you were out.

So it should be in tomorrow's edition.' Julia sounded very pleased with herself. 'I knew you wouldn't remember, Max, but these things are important.'

Max paled. The world had gone mad! Or rather *his* world had gone mad. His colleagues at the office would be laughing their collective socks off when they heard he was engaged. His partner, Richard, always called him the last bachelor in London, his antipathy towards marriage was so well-known.

Thea set down the tray of drinks she was carrying on the low coffee table. Her hair had escaped from the plait she had been wearing and was floating in golden wisps around her face, the light from the window making it gleam in the evening sun.

She looked tired, Max noticed guiltily. She had worked hard getting the house ready for them all, cooking and cleaning everywhere.

Refocusing on the conversation, he realised Julia was asking Thea about her family, if there was anyone she wanted to ask to the dinner party.

'My mother died when I was a teenager and I lost my father a few months ago. There isn't anyone else.' Her blue eyes clouded and Max wished he was sitting close enough to hug her and chase the sad expression away.

'I'm sorry.' Julia bit her lower lip. 'We lost our dad a few years ago too, not along after he and our mother finally divorced. Mother lives in Australia now, with husband number four.'

Thea couldn't hide her surprise. 'I didn't know.'

'We don't hear from her very often. Unless she wants money or a favour.' Max hadn't intended to sound so harsh but from the look on Thea's face he knew she had noted the bitterness in his tone.

'She's only ever seen Emily once and that was when she was born. She doesn't like to think of herself as being old enough to be a grandmother,' Julia explained.

'That's so sad. She's missed out on such a lot.'

Max could see Thea was completely perplexed by his mother's attitude to Emily.

'Mother doesn't see it like that,' he put in. 'She only kept up the loving parent act long enough to win custody of us from Dad, then she dumped us at boarding-school while she went off on her merry way.'

His eyes met Thea's and he could read the reflection of his own pain in their clear blue depths. Only a choky little sigh from Julia broke the silence.

'I'm just going to check on Emily.' Julia bolted into the hall with a stricken face, leaving Thea and Max alone in the lounge.

Thea looked concerned. 'Do you think we should go after her?'

'It's best to leave her alone. Julia has never really accepted Mother's total lack of interest ·in either of us as anything other than a weapon to beat Dad with. That's why this trouble between her and Paul has hit her so hard.'

'And why she worries so much about Emily?' Thea questioned softly.

Max sighed; how had this conversation got started? The air in the room seemed to weigh down on his lungs, making it hard to breathe, and he knew he had to get outside. Running away? his brain asked.

He stood up abruptly. 'I need to go outside, get some fresh air.'

Thea appeared to hesitate before asking, 'Would you like company?'

He nodded, not trusting himself to speak.

She uncoiled herself from where she had been sitting with her legs tucked beneath her on the settee and followed him outside.

Max wasn't sure where he was going; all he knew was that he needed fresh air and open space. Any discussion involving his parents' doomed marriage had the same effect on him now as it had when he was an adolescent.

Thea seemed to understand, and walked companionably at his side without speaking while he marshalled the mixture of emotions whirling around inside his head into some sort of order.

Thea was thinking hard. A lot of pieces of the complicated puzzle of Max's life appeared to be coming together. No wonder he held such strong views against love and marriage. She could see, too, why he was so willing to put himself through this crazy deception for Emily's and Julia's sakes.

She didn't care to look too closely at her own motivations for going along with it, however much she might try to convince herself it was merely the need to repair Stony Gables.

'One of these days, Thea, you'll take on more than you can handle.' Her father's words resonated in her mind. Over the years a procession of people and animals had found their way to Stony Gables courtesy of Thea's tender heart.

Fred the rooster and his harem of lady chickens had arrived after their elderly owner had been taken to hospital. Then there was the three-legged cat that no one had wanted, and even Mr Smith, the well-dressed bear in the hall, had been rescued from a skip. She smiled to herself as she remembered cycling home with the huge bear tied to her back.

'This way.' They had reached the end of the path, so Thea led the way over the stile into the field. The shady riverside walk was one of her favourite places and she had spent many happy hours in her childhood sitting on the low stone bridge farther upstream which spanned the shallow water.

The evening sun was sending rays of golden light between the branches and in the fields the rabbits began to emerge cautiously out into the long grass to hop about.

'It's so quiet here.' Max, too, watched the wildlife as they strolled along, side by side.

'Apart from the birds,' Thea teased. The birds were kicking off the evening chorus and down by the water's edge the sound magnified into a symphony of birdsong.

'I'm sorry I dragged you into all this, Thea.' He glanced at her, his dark eyes giving nothing away.

She offered him a half smile. 'I don't recall being dragged.'

'Well, maybe dragged is the wrong word, but you know what I mean.'

They stopped by the stone bridge and Thea sat herself down on the edge, her legs dangling over the water which gurgled and splashed below.

'My father always used to tell me I was a sucker for a sob story,' she confided.

Max seated himself beside her on the bridge and picked idly at the yellow lichen on the top of the masonry.

'Is that why you're doing this? Because you feel sorry for us?'

Thea sensed she was going to have to tread very carefully.

'I need your rent money to make repairs to Stony Gables. You've probably noticed some of the plumbing is a little on the ancient side, not to mention the paintwork needs doing and the roof chimneys need repair.' She sighed at the thought of the costs involved.

Max flicked a small pebble into the stream below.

'I'm glad you don't see me as a charity case.'

He probably thought she was a real hard-hearted Annie now.

One of these days, Thea Sinclair, she thought to herself, you have got to learn a bit of tact. She always managed to say or do the wrong thing whenever she was in a one-to-one situation with an eligible man.

Not that Max is an eligible man, she backtracked hastily, he was just a . . . She glanced at him and found her brain was having trouble deciding exactly *what* kind of man Max was, if he wasn't eligible. Too nice-looking for his own good, she thought wryly. Too nice-looking for *her* good.

Conscious that she was staring, she dropped her gaze to concentrate on the patterns in the water where it flowed over the stones of the riverbed.

'Are the repairs the reason Henry was putting so much pressure on you at Ginny's dinner party?'

Thea hadn't realised Max had heard so much of that evening's conversation.

'When my father died, the house had to be valued as part of the estate. Henry saw the surveyor's report and obviously he realised that if he can persuade me to sell, there's a substantial profit to be made.' She scowled.

'Charming man, your friend Henry.' Max's fingers brushed against hers where she was gripping the edge of the stonework.

'He's all heart.' To her surprise her voice sounded breathy and her blood was pounding in her veins.

Max traced a lazy finger along the line of her jaw to tilt her face, so that she was forced to lift her head and look into the deep chocolate brown of his eyes.

His lips grazed hers, sending a shiver of delight through her before his mouth claimed possession. Only her precarious position on the parapet of the bridge kept her grounded as her body responded to his, melting away all her good intentions about keeping her distance.

The sound of children's voices in the distance broke the spell and as Max lifted his head, she saw the shutters close over his emotions and knew he was already regretting giving in to the impulse to kiss her.

Shakily she took a deep breath. Two could play at that game. Pride pushed her to act as though nothing had happened.

'We'd better go back to the house. Julia will wonder where we've got to and I need to see to the chickens.' She slid down from the bridge, spurning the hand he offered to help her.

Max found Julia in the kitchen making a cup of tea. Her eyes were pink around the rims and her usually neat hairstyle looked uncharacteristically tousled.

'Where's Thea?' she asked.

'She stopped by the run to take care of the chickens.' He hesitated. He didn't know what to say to his sister to make her feel better. He hadn't known what to say to Thea down by the river, either.

The thought occurred to him that Thea would know exactly what to say to Julia. Thea had a real gift for talking to people, and her easy tactile nature made her good company to have around. Unless, like now, she was mad at him.

Julia sniffed and concentrated on pouring her tea. 'Would you like a cup?'

'I'd love one.' he said, and reached for one of the big, brightly-painted mugs that stood all along the top of the dresser.

Julia poured him some tea and went to the fridge for the milk.

'I made a list of guests for you and Thea to invite to the dinner party. It's really only Ginny and Laurence, me, and some of the staff from our office. I didn't think Thea would want to meet any of your old flames.'

'It's a little late for that.' He could have bitten his tongue off as soon as he'd said the words. Julia's face lit up with interest and she set the milk bottle back down on the table with a thud, a single drop plopping out on to the surface.

'You never said anything about that. Who was it and when?'

Max resigned himself to the inevitable and told Julia about bumping into Gabby in the high street. Julia pursed her lips when she heard that Gabby had rented a property in the village.

'I wouldn't have thought there was much to interest her in the country-side.'

While Gabby and his sister had met a

few times socially, Max knew that Julia hadn't been impressed by her.

For some reason, although Gabby had always appeared to be very nice to Julia, the feeling had never been reciprocated. Yet Max had always thought they should have had a lot in common. Like Julia, Gabby was attractive, intelligent and well-groomed, with good social connections.

If anything, it was Julia's meeting with Thea that Max had had misgivings about. Thea's wild hair, unconventional habits and fashion sense should have meant Julia disapproving of her on sight, but instead the two of them seemed to really like each other.

Julia put the milk back in the fridge and yawned widely.

'Well, I'm going to have an early night. This country air's making me sleepy. Say goodnight to Thea for me, will you?'

Max gave her an affectionate goodnight peck on the cheek and sat down at the old pine table to wait for Thea.

When she came in from dealing with the chickens they had to figure out what they were going to do about the sleeping arrangements for the night ahead.

Hatching The Plot

Thea deliberately took her time down by the chicken run. What on earth was she going to do about tonight? If she was honest with herself, she had to admit that Max definitely appealed to her senses, and when he touched her, she fizzed up inside like a firework. But how were they going to manage without him noticing how he made her feel? Her cheeks grew warm as her mind replayed the images of Max when he had stripped off his wet clothes in her kitchen the day he had arrived.

As she reached the back door, she took a deep breath. 'You are a grown woman, Theodora Sinclair. It's not like you haven't seen a nearly nude man before, so get a grip!'

Intent on going straight to the sink to wash her hands, she didn't bother to switch on the light.

'I thought you'd decided to stay down in the henhouse for the night with Fred instead of coming back here.'

Thea jumped. In the darkness she hadn't noticed Max sitting at the table.

'You startled me!' Drying her hands quickly on the towel, she reached over and flicked the electric light switch.

'I'm sorry, I didn't mean to make you jump. Julia's gone up to bed. She said to wish you goodnight.'

Thea wished her heart would stop racing. Being alone with Max was too disturbing. Since he had kissed her down by the stream she felt as jumpy as a kitten.

'I thought you'd be in the lounge, watching TV or something.' She hoped he hadn't heard her giving herself that little pep talk outside the door.

'I thought I'd wait for you to come in. It was getting dark outside, so I wanted to make sure you were all right.'

The husky note of concern in his voice fused her brain. It was a long time since a man had shown any consideration for her welfare and the intensity of Max's gaze was making her feel quite flustered.

'Had any good ideas about this room-sharing business?' His dark eyes locked on to her face.

She licked her lips nervously. 'Erm, I . . . ' Her voice sounded suspiciously squeaky and she wished he would stop looking at her like that. 'Well, sort of. You'll be a bit cramped but I think it'll work.'

Max sighed. 'I guess that means we're using another of your famous plans.'

'What do you mean?' Her throat was as dry and scratchy as sandpaper and her stomach felt as if it were playing host to a ballroom full of butterflies.

Max leaned back in his chair and locked his hands behind his head. He was still watching her closely. 'I think we have to go with the *wing it* option,' he said softly.

Uncomfortable under his gaze, she

turned and filled the kettle from the tap, all too conscious of her rosy cheeks. She set the kettle on the hot plate and hoped he hadn't noticed her hands shaking.

He pushed his chair aside and took his empty mug over to the Aga.

'If you're making tea, I could use another cup,' he said.

The air between them crackled with invisible energy.

'Thea, I know this is hard on you and I want to tell you how much I appreciate everything you're doing to help us. I was out of line earlier when we were by the river, but it's been an unusual day. Now — what's this plan you've come up with?'

The kettle started to whistle and her hands shook as she picked up the pot-holder to lift it off the plate. She was relieved when she managed to pour water on to the teabags without spilling it everywhere.

'Well, like you said this morning, if we're going to be convincing, then I guess we have to look the part — although it's not my way. I intend to wait till I'm married for . . . that sort of thing.' She felt herself blushing.

Max nodded in understanding, a light of admiration in his eyes. 'Fair enough. So what's this plan?'

'In my room there's a walk-in closet. I think if I rearrange some things, you could sleep in there. It's not very big and there's no window, but it'll do.'

Max added the milk to the mugs and stirred the tea. 'OK, I'll give it a go. We just have to keep remembering that all this pretence is for Emily's sake. So — do you want to go up first and get ready? There's a programme I'd like to catch on TV.'

Thea knew he was trying to make the whole business as painless as possible for her and she appreciated his thoughtfulness, but the comment about remembering their engagement was pretence stung. After all, he had kissed her first, so perhaps it was him who needed to remember it was all pretend!

'I'll see you later then,' she said and shot upstairs, mentally scolding herself for being too cowardly to challenge him about that kiss.

* * *

The air in her bedroom was still and heavy and even with the sash window pushed up as far as it would go, there wasn't a breath of wind to stir the soft cotton fabric of the curtains.

Julia had placed Max's bag and his clothes on the old wicker rocking chair that stood in the corner of the room. Thea's room was one of the bedrooms most in need of decorating. The wallpaper was old and faded, with a mark under the window where the damp came through in the winter. Lack of space meant her double bed was pushed up against the wall with just a narrow strip of threadbare carpet showing between it and the door.

She placed her mug carefully on top of the dresser and looked despondently around the room. There wasn't a lot of space for her in there, let alone squeezing all six-foot-three of Max in as well. She wondered how long he was going to be downstairs.

The closet was musty which was why she didn't use it to store her clothes. She opened the door cautiously and peered in. The last time she'd gone in there to find something a huge spider had run out and gone under her bed and she'd had to spend half an hour hunting it down to get rid of it before she could go to sleep.

Eying the narrow floor space, she reckoned if she moved the junk most of Max would fit in. If he hadn't been so tall it wouldn't have been as difficult. He would have to have the door open and sleep with his feet sticking out into her room.

Moving quietly so as not to disturb Julia, whose room was just across the corridor, she carefully moved the boxes of photographs and bric-a-brac out of the closet and on to the top of her wardrobe, keeping her eyes open all the time in case another spider was lurking. Once everything was safely shifted she crept over to the blue room and sneaked some bedding back to her own room. Fortunately for Max one of the things in the cupboard was an ancient camp-bed, so at least he wouldn't be forced to lie on the floorboards.

She felt so hot and sticky after making up the camp-bed and moving her possessions, it would be heaven to dive into her little bathroom and take a shower. There was no lock on the bedroom door though, and the bolt on the bathroom had so many layers of paint over it she doubted if it would ever draw, and the thought that Max might walk in on her sent her thoughts scattering in all directions.

Remembering that she couldn't shut Max in the cupboard she made a snap decision and rummaged in a drawer for something suitable to wear in bed.

'A girl has her pride,' she muttered, stuffing her shortie nightshirt with the sad puppy picture on the front to the bottom of the pile.

Finally she emerged triumphant with a pretty broderie-anglaise vest-style top and matching pyjama bottoms. An unworn Christmas gift from a few years ago, she eyed them up in the lamplight and hoped they would still fit.

Standing under the lukewarm shower in her tiny bathroom, she tried to listen out for Max coming upstairs. She had to get dried and in her nightclothes before he arrived or she would never be able to look him in the face again.

Much to her relief, the camisole set still fitted. At least she looked decent, and the set was fairly cool to wear.

She smiled to herself, willing to bet her last pound that Gabby didn't wear a cartoon print nightshirt in bed.

★   ★   ★

Max couldn't concentrate on the television. He flicked between the channels trying to judge when would be the best time to go upstairs to Thea's room. He hoped she would be in her bed and fast asleep when he got there. That way he could creep in quietly and it would probably be less embarrassing for both of them.

It was typical of Julia to land them in this mess, although to be fair, if they hadn't deceived her in the first place it wouldn't have been a problem.

His thoughts lingered on Thea. She was the marrying kind. But he wasn't, and it would be cruel to lead her on when he could make her no promises. He really shouldn't have kissed her earlier. However much they both tried to pretend that it was all part of an act, he knew from the look in Thea's eyes when his lips had touched hers that the spark of attraction he felt towards her was more than reciprocated.

No matter how hard this room-sharing was going to be, he owed it to her not to make her feel uncomfortable. He shifted restlessly in the armchair. He had the feeling it was going to be a long and sleepless night.

As he undressed quietly in the dark, stripping off his jeans and shirt, keeping just his boxer shorts on, Max thought Thea was asleep.

It was so hot, as if all the heat in the house had risen during the day to settle in this one small room. In the dim light he could see the door of the closet standing open and the end of the camp-bed sticking out.

In his efforts to keep quiet and not disturb her, he tripped over his shoe and stubbed his toe on the camp-bed. He muttered under his breath as Thea rolled over to face him, her expression unreadable in the dim light.

'I'm sorry; I was trying not to disturb you.' He sat down on the edge of her bed and rubbed his toe.

'It's OK, I was awake anyway. It's so hot tonight.'

He wondered if she felt as awkward as he did. 'I'll just go and get in then . . . '

'If you want to sleep tonight, you don't have much choice,' she agreed.

'What do you think they would have done in this situation in Victorian times?' he mused as he inched his way cautiously onto the camp-bed and prayed it would take his weight. It didn't feel particularly sturdy.

The canvas creaked under him and he held his breath.

'Didn't they used to put a bolster — one of those long, lumpy pillows — down the middle of the bed? In between the couple?' she suggested.

He could make out her features now in the moonlight. Her eyes were watching him, dark and mysterious.

'Got a bolster handy? This thing feels a bit rickety.'

She gurgled with laughter. 'No bolsters. You're staying right there, mister. Do you think Julia would notice if we got Mr Smith to chaperone?'

'I think Emily would notice if he went walkabout. She's really taken with that old bear.' Thea's toe-ring gleamed in the moonlight as she wriggled her bare foot free from under the sheet. He guessed her joking was her way of hiding her nervousness.

'Are you OK down there? I'm afraid you might be uncomfortable,' she ventured.

'I'll manage, don't worry.'

Max could feel little beads of perspiration trickling down his back. He was hot, tired and uncomfortable, and the cupboard was airless, but he wouldn't let her know it.

'Goodnight then, Max.'

She gazed out of the window at the stars twinkling away in the deep blue velvet of the night sky. Max made a peculiar, muffled groaning noise as he adjusted his position on the camp bed. She hoped he didn't snore.

This was crazy. *She* was crazy.

She twisted a strand of her hair around her finger, thinking. Max was an attractive man. OK, so he was a *very* attractive man, and he was a good kisser. He loved his sister and his little niece. He was kind, caring — darn it, he was perfect!

He was the kind of man she had always dreamed of meeting, except he didn't believe in marriage, commitment and all the values that she held to be important. He was afraid to risk his heart, to open himself to any kind of relationship that wasn't merely superficial. She had made the mistake in the past of confusing attraction with love and she wasn't going to go down that route again.

She sighed softly. Trust her to be attracted to Mr Commitment-phobe. She twiddled the alien weight of the engagement ring round on her finger. Maybe he might change his mind . . .

'Thea, not everyone feels the way you do. You have to accept that you can't change everyone.' Her father had counselled her on so many occasions when one of her ducks failed yet again to turn into a swan. Her eyes filled with tears; sometimes she still missed him so much.

★ ★ ★

The sound of someone moving around in her room woke Thea the next morning. Opening her eyes carefully she was treated to a view of Max wearing just his boxers attempting to stuff the camp bed and the bedding away out of sight inside the closet.

'Morning,' she mumbled.

He turned at the sound of her voice. 'I'm sorry; I didn't mean to wake you.' He gave the bed a last push and shut the cupboard door just as they heard the sound of small feet running along the landing, then the bedroom door burst open and Emily ran into the room. Her arms were full of dolls and teddy bears which she flung on to the covers. Climbing up after the toys, she wriggled into bed beside Thea and beamed happily at their startled faces.

'Morning, Uncle Max — morning, Thea. Do you want to play with me? Mummy's still asleep and it's all sunny and nice outside.'

It took Thea a moment to pull herself together enough to answer.

'Tell you what, Emily — how about Uncle Max making me a cup of tea and getting you a mug of milk, and later on, after breakfast, he can come down to the river with us and we'll see if we can catch some fish?' It would give Thea the breathing space she needed to compose herself.

Emily clapped her hands together with delight. 'Go on, Uncle Max. It'll be lots of fun.' Her big brown eyes were shining with excitement.

Max sighed and reached for his jeans.

'Actually, Max, Emily and I'll have breakfast in bed this morning. You'll find the trays in the bottom of the dresser. Toast and jam will be lovely.' She smiled sweetly at him, though the sight of him bare-chested with his hair tousled and a faint line of stubble on his jaw was wreaking havoc with her pulse rate.

'Can we really have breakfast up here in bed?' Emily asked. 'Mummy won't let me at home; she says it makes a mess.'

'Well, now you're on holiday and this is a special treat to start your stay,' Thea reassured her and smiled when the little girl beamed and began arranging her toys on the bed ready for the unexpected treat.

Max looked at Thea as if he would have liked to say something, but instead he slipped out of the bedroom and she heard his footsteps pad away down the stairs. Her mind whirred all the while he was gone as Emily busily chattered to her teddy bears.

How come Max was having this effect on her? And more importantly, why did she like it so much? It was the answer to the last question which was trying her the most.

Max came back upstairs a few minutes later carrying a wooden tray with little extendable legs.

'Tea, toast and jam, my ladies.' He flipped the legs open and set the tray down carefully on the bed. Thea noticed it was only set for two.

Emily beat her to the punch. 'Aren't

you eating breakfast, Uncle Max?'

Max smiled. 'If I'm to go fishing with you and Thea later, then I have to go downstairs and get some work done first.'

He rummaged in his bag for a few things. 'I'll use the other bathroom, it'll be quicker.'

'Fine. Emily and I'll be down later,' Thea announced.

As Max moved towards the door, Emily wriggled off the bed, narrowly managing to avoid upending the breakfast tray, and held up her arms. 'I want a kiss.'

Max grinned. 'I'm only going for a shower and to get my work done.' He ruffled Emily's hair and stooped to kiss the top of her head.

'You haven't kissed Thea,' Emily pointed out accusingly, as Max's hand reached for the door knob.

Thea's heart skipped a beat as he turned and came back to where she was sitting propped up on the pillows. His eyes met hers and he kissed her gently on the lips. Then he was gone and Emily was clambering back on to the bed.

'I love Uncle Max, don't you, Thea?'

Thea stared shakily at the closed bedroom door. 'Yes, I think maybe I do, Emily,' she answered slowly and this time she wasn't faking it.

The Sweetest Kiss

Max stood in the shower, scrubbing fiercely at his skin with the soap. He had to put some distance between himself and Thea. Emily's innocent reminder to kiss his 'fiancée' had almost finished him.

He closed his eyes and let the warm water trickle down between his shoulder blades. He had to find a good excuse to escape for a few hours, something that wouldn't arouse Julia's suspicions.

He turned off the water and reached for a towel. He needed a few hours back in his own world, away from the crazy Alice-In-Wonderland effect this house and Thea were having on him.

As he moved to grab his jeans from the bathroom chair, he spotted his excuse. Clothes — that was it. He needed to move more of his clothes down here. He couldn't keep wearing the few things he had brought with him.

Padding over to the mirror, he got out his shaving kit. He could spend the morning fishing with Emily and then go back to London and pack up some more of his things. Perfect!

★ ★ ★

After breakfast, Thea packed a simple picnic lunch into a wicker hamper.

Julia cried off the fishing trip to make phone calls and sort out last-minute details before leaving for Singapore, while Max stayed closeted in the study for much of the morning, so Thea spent her time supervising Emily and think-ing over her feelings.

'Uncle Max!' Emily slipped down from where she was kneeling on a chair at Thea's side and rushed across the room as he emerged from the study. 'Thea's made a picnic, we're going to take nets down to the stream and paddle in the water while we catch fish.'

Max swung her up into his arms. 'Sounds like fun.'

He tried to recall the last time he'd been on a picnic. It was probably the annual school picnic just before he had left boarding-school for college. Memories flooded back: the smell of the grass, the freshly-painted white lines on the running track, the familiar sick feeling when he realised yet again that there was no-one there to watch him race.

One of his school traditions had been for all the boys' families to be invited for a founder's day celebration every June. There was a mass picnic, sports, and a tour of the school. His mother had never attended because the date usually clashed with several others in her busy social calendar, and by then his father had been too ill. He had never been on this kind of picnic, a simple family outing. There had never been any family outings at all.

'Where's Julia?' He had only seen his

sister fleetingly, when she had popped into the study to mouth something at him about inviting his colleagues for the dinner party tomorrow.

'She's busy sorting out a few things for when she leaves.' Thea fastened the hamper and smiled at Emily. 'So we're going to give her some peace while we go and have fun.'

A loud clanking noise sounded from the front door. Emily put her hands over her ears and Thea went to see who was ringing the bell.

'Hi, Thea. You couldn't do me a favour and have Tom for me, could you? I know it's short notice but Laurence is desperately short of staff at the surgery this morning and he has to meet the planners later, so I've promised to look in.' Ginny looked frazzled. Tom stood at her side, hopping hopefully from one foot to the other.

'I wouldn't ask, but Laurence really could use my help.' There was an unaccustomed note of panic in Ginny's voice. The last time Thea could remember her friend getting this anxious was when she had been pregnant with Tom. Laurence must really need her help for her to be so flustered.

'No problem — he'll be company for Emily. We're going fishing in the stream and having a picnic.' Thea never minded looking after Tom. She loved his funny ways and it would be nice for Emily to have a playmate.

Tom let out a whoop of delight and Ginny sighed with relief. 'I'll be back as soon as I can. I really appreciate this, Thea.'

Tom had already gone to the kitchen and was busy telling Emily about the delights of the river when Thea joined them.

'I gather we've an extra one?' Max nodded towards Tom.

'Ginny has to go and help Laurence at the surgery. I think it's a bit of a crisis.'

She gathered up the towels and picnic things. 'Right, have we got everything? Sunhats, sun cream?' she asked.

Emily and Tom nodded eagerly, their baseball-capped heads bobbing up and down.

'Can I get the nets from the hall?' Tom was bouncing about by the door.

'I'll help.' Emily was keen to assist.

The two children trotted off to collect the fishing nets, coming back in seconds with two small nets on long poles and a couple of brightly-coloured plastic buckets. Tom had also perched the Panama hat which belonged to Mr Smith, the bear, on top of his baseball cap.

Seeing Max's puzzled expression, Thea whisked the hat from Tom and popped it on her own head at a jaunty angle.

'Mr Smith lends it to me for expeditions, otherwise I get a pink and peeling nose,' she explained, attempting to look dignified and wishing she had something a little more flattering to wear.

Laden down with bags, they called goodbye to Julia and set off down the long path to the river. Tom and Emily ran on a little way ahead. Thea could see the nets bobbing about wildly in the air and hear the distant sound of their childish laughter.

Max fell into step beside her. 'I have to go back to London later today. I need to move more of my things down here and there's a couple of things I need to check up on at work.'

Thea peeped at him from under the brim of her hat. 'Will you be away long?'

Really, she wanted to know if he was going to be gone overnight, but she couldn't bring herself to be so direct.

'It depends. I might have to stay over.' His voice was studiously neutral.

Suddenly the bright sunny morning seemed to lose some of its charm for Thea, and ludicrously, she couldn't help feeling disappointed.

At the end of the day though, Max was employing her to do a job. He was hiring her home and her skills as a nanny, and however lovely his kisses might be and however nice it was to play make-believe, the truth was, he wasn't in the market to play happy families for real. If he found out she was harbouring any kind of romantic feelings towards him, the whole thing would become a disaster.

'Tom! Keep to the path and watch the nettles,' she called as the erratic fishing nets bobbed temporarily out of sight.

Max offered her his hand to climb over the stile. The touch of his lean, strong fingers in her palm was an agony of delight.

They followed the children along a different path from the previous night, following a small tributary leading away from the main river.

The path narrowed to a walkway only wide enough for one person at a time as it wound its way between tall, swishing clumps of grass. Thea had to walk in front of Max until the track opened out into a small meadow where the stream gurgled, shallow and flat, between large rocks.

Tom was already standing at the edge of the bank, leaning perilously over the water and pointing out something to Emily. As soon as they saw Thea and Max, both children came scampering over, breathless with excitement to tell about what they had seen.

'I saw a fish, Uncle Max! A real one. He's down there by the rocks. Tom says we can paddle and go and catch him and — ' Emily couldn't get her words out quickly enough.

Max looked at Thea. 'Is it safe for them to paddle?'

Tom had already pulled his socks and shoes off, and Max knelt to pick them up.

'Perfectly — it's very shallow here. The water's cold, though.' She helped Emily take off her socks and sandals. 'Why don't you go and join them while I set out the rugs for the picnic?' The two children were already shrieking and splashing in the water, and she smiled. 'I guess any fish within a two-mile radius will have disappeared by now.'

Max was gazing at Tom and Emily as they paddled ankle-deep in the stream, picking their way over the pebbles that littered the bottom.

'Max?' Thea prompted. He seemed lost in a world of his own.

He turned to her and blinked. 'I've never done this kind of thing before.' He sounded lost and uncertain, his usual confidence gone as he glanced back at the children in the stream.

Thea swallowed. She guessed it had cost him a lot in pride to make that kind of admission. He was uncomfortable whenever it came to talking about his past.

'You never went on picnics?' she asked gently.

He shook his head and pulled absentmindedly at a blade of grass. Thea's heart lurched. She longed to pull him into her arms and hold him tight, seeing in the tough man the hurt little boy he had once been.

'The only times we ever went anywhere as a family were when Mother deemed it an important social occasion. You know — weddings, christenings, stuff like that.'

Thea looked across at the children playing happily together in the shallow water.

'That's why we need to make things different for Emily,' she said softly. 'That's why we're going through this whole fake engagement. So that she won't grow up with those kinds of unhappy memories.' Instinctively she placed her hand over his.

Max's hand stilled in hers and for a fleeting second she glimpsed the raw emotion in his eyes before he drew away and rose to his feet, brushing blades of grass from his jeans.

As he walked away towards the stream, Max struggled to fit the lid back on the memories of his childhood. He glanced back at Thea, sitting on the rug under the tree, her long legs, bare below her shorts, dappled by the shade of the leaves and her pretty face hidden from view under her ridiculous hat.

Kicking off his trainers and socks, he ventured into the stream. Tom and Emily roared with laughter at his expression when the cold water lapped around his ankles.

'Uncle Max, come and help me catch a fish.' Emily handed him one of the brightly-coloured plastic buckets as she balanced on one of the flat grey stones which protruded above the surface of the water.

Thea walked down to the edge of the stream. 'Smile everyone — I want to take some pictures.'

Emily grinned happily as she posed for a photo while Tom pulled funny faces.

'I didn't know you'd brought a camera,' Max said, wading towards her.

'I thought Julia might like to take some pictures with her, or she can email them to Paul before she goes. I expect he's missing Emily and this way he'll see that she's happy and enjoying herself.'

Max's heart gave a squeeze. He hadn't thought of how Paul might be feeling. If he were Emily's father, he would want to know she was safe and happy.

He caught himself up with that thought. He wasn't a father and never planned to be.

'Can you still feel your feet?' Thea teased, looking at where he was standing in the icy water.

Shaking his head, he climbed out of the stream on to the grassy bank. Thea was still smiling at him, her blue eyes warm and compassionate.

'Come and get a towel to dry yourself off. I'll give the children a few more minutes then we'll have lunch.'

Thea walked away, back towards the shade of the tree, and Max took a moment to admire her in her shorts. She was so pretty . . .

He bit his lip and flung himself down on the rug. Seizing a towel, he rubbed fiercely at his wet feet, picking off the stray bits of grass that were stuck to his skin.

Thea began to unpack the contents of the hamper, fetching out bottles of fruit juice for the children, who rushed over as soon as they noticed that the picnic hamper was open.

'We're starving, aren't we, Emily? Oh wow, watermelon!' Tom plunged a hand into the basket then, catching sight of Thea's mock severe frown, withdrew it, looking guilty.

Thea laughed and started to share out the food from the hamper. Max watched her thoughtfully as she joked and played with Emily and Tom whilst he ate the delicious crusty bread and fresh cheese she had provided. Julia's comment about Thea making a wonderful mother floated back into his mind and began to niggle away at his subconscious.

With the warm sun and the country air, he soon found his eyelids were growing heavy. Tom went back down to the stream to look for fish while Emily and Thea made daisy chains on the rug. Closing his eyes, Max lay back in the sunshine and allowed himself to relax . . .

★ ★ ★

It seemed like only minutes later that he could hear Emily giggling and Thea's soft voice shushing her as something tickled his chin. He opened his eyes to see Thea's laughing face close to his as she held something tickly by his neck.

'What are you . . . ' He struggled to sit up and discovered he was festooned in daisy chains. Emily was helpless with mirth, rolling around on the rug roaring with laughter till she gave herself hiccups.

'Sorry, Max. We couldn't resist it.' Thea was as bad as Emily, her face wreathed in a smile as open and sunny as the afternoon. Max grinned. He guessed he must look pretty funny.

'We were just testing to see if you like butter.' Emily hiccupped and pointed to the buttercup in Thea's hand. 'You hold it under your chin and if your chin goes all yellow then you like butter,' she explained helpfully.

Max took the flower from Thea. 'Like this?' he asked, holding the tiny flower under Thea's chin. Her eyes became large and wide. The sweet fullness of her mouth drew him like a magnet as he moved the buttercup away. Suddenly her lips were meeting his with a sigh and he lost all sense of where he was . . .

'Ugh, kissing! Yuk!' Tom had come up from the stream to see what all the laughter was about and was pulling disgusted faces at them.

Thea immediately turned very pink and flustered, gabbling about having been there long enough and how they should go back to the house in case Ginny had arrived to fetch Tom.

★　★　★

Thea suspected Max hadn't been entirely truthful when he had told her why he needed to return to London. All the same, perhaps a break from one another's company might not be a bad idea. Max's kisses played havoc with her heart.

Max had made light of Tom's teasing by chasing him and pretending to throw him in the stream, a game which Emily soon begged to join in. Thankfully Thea had been left in peace to pack up the picnic things and compose her feelings before they all walked back to the house.

The emerald ring on her engagement finger was winking accusingly at her as they made their way along the path. How could she have been so stupid as to allow her feelings to become involved with a man who had repeatedly warned her that he didn't do 'happy ever after'?

Maybe she was plain stupid. Her father and Ginny had both warned her often enough in the past about allowing her heart to rule her head. She glanced along the path ahead, where Max was comparing strides with Tom. There had been a few boyfriends in her past who she had thought might turn out to be 'the one', but invariably, as soon as she had started to think that way, they had made the 'let's be friends' speech.

'Thea, when the right man for you comes along, you'll know it,' Ginny had once counselled her as she had dried her tears after yet another disastrous date. 'You get too serious too soon. Life isn't like the movies, not everything has a happy ending.'

Thea knew Ginny was right, though she didn't like to think she was that naive. Yet she had fallen head over heels for Jon, her last boyfriend. Until her father's illness, she had been sure that he really was the one. If he had proposed to her back then she would have accepted in a heartbeat, and she had been sure he *was* planning to propose. It just went to show how wrong you could be about someone. When her father had become ill and it had been obvious that he couldn't continue to live on his own, Jon had shown his true colours:

'Thea, you can't give up everything and go home! Can't someone else look after him? Surely there are hospices and places like that where he could go and be looked after?'

Jon's only concern had been how her decision would affect him. There had been no thought for how she had felt seeing her beloved father slowly losing his memory and dignity to Alzheimer's, the illness that had finally robbed him of his life.

What was wrong with wanting to find a partner to love and who would love her for the rest of her life? Someone to grow old with, to raise a family with? Jon had been so selfish, and so cold. She stared unhappily at Max's back. How had she managed to fall for Mr Wrong yet again, and more heavily than she had ever thought possible?

Julia and Ginny were sitting on the wooden bench outside the back door of the house. A quick glance at Julia's face told Thea that she had been crying again. Ginny looked tired and pale too, although her face lit up as the children came racing along the path towards them. Julia also brightened perceptibly as Emily sat down next to her and started to tell her about the day's adventures.

Sitting down on one of the chairs next to the bench, Thea fanned herself with the Panama hat. Even with Max carrying the picnic hamper, it had still been a hot walk from the riverside.

'I think we could all use a drink,' Max suggested and took the hamper into the house, reappearing a few minutes later with a tray full of glasses and a large jug of fruit juice.

'Did you have a nice time?' Julia asked, as he placed the tray on the rickety wooden table.

'They were kissing!' Tom announced in tones of deepest disgust.

Julia laughed but Ginny looked at Thea and raised an enquiring eyebrow.

'Sounds to me like a successful outing,' Julia said.

'Yes, doesn't it?' Ginny added meaningly, and Thea's face burned.

Max glanced at his watch. 'I'd better shower and change if I'm to make it back to London tonight in time to call in at work.'

Julia frowned. 'Surely you don't have to go back now? Emily and I have only just arrived and already you're dashing off.'

'I need to move some more of my things down here, and I have a couple of things to attend to at the office. I'll only be gone overnight.'

'You'd better be! It's your engagement dinner tomorrow, remember, and I'd like to see a little more of you before I have to leave.' Julia didn't look happy.

Thea picked up her glass and swirled it to make the ice cubes spin. However, lifting the tumbler to her lips to take a sip, she almost choked on the contents at Julia's next suggestion:

'Well, if you're going to be there

overnight, why don't you take Thea with you? You could go out to dinner or see a show. Emily and I'll be fine here till you get back. It would be a nice break for you both.' Julia relaxed back happily on the bench and smiled at them. 'You won't get much time alone together once I've gone, so think of it as a child-free respite. Trust me, you'll need it.'

Thea was conscious of Ginny watching her as she coughed on her juice. She replaced her glass on the table with a hand that wasn't quite steady.

'That's a nice thought, Julia, but I couldn't. I mean, there's the chickens and . . . '

'Oh, I can take care of Fred and his girlfriends,' Ginny piped up. 'I agree with Julia — it would give you both a break and Julia and I can have a nice girly evening together.'

Thea stared at her. What was going on? Ginny knew this engagement was a put-up job, so why was she pushing them together?

'I was only going to pack up a few more things and call in at the office. There won't be much time for anything else,' Max protested.

He didn't want her tagging along, Thea realised. His expression suggested he would rather have his teeth drilled than take her to London with him.

'Nonsense! You can always pop out to that little Italian restaurant round the corner from your apartment and have dinner.' Julia looked at her brother closely. 'Anyone would think you didn't want Thea to go with you.'

'Of course I want her to come. I just thought it would be a bit boring for her.'

To Thea's ears, his protestations sounded hollow and she swallowed the feeling of disappointment that he didn't want her company. Julia, however, seemed satisfied with his response.

'Well, you'd better go and pack a few things, Thea, if you two are going to miss the traffic,' Ginny added, sipping her drink.

'Will you bring me back a present?' Tom had been stalking a butterfly with the fishing net while they had been talking and Thea hadn't realised he'd been listening to the conversation.

The general laughter that greeted the question appeared to dispel some of the tension that Thea could feel emanating from Max.

'We'd better go and pack then.' Max placed his glass on the tray and walked around to stand behind Thea, his hand coming to rest on her bare shoulder. A ripple of awareness spread from the cool touch of his fingers over her warm skin.

Struggling with her composure, Thea tried to play her part. 'If you two are sure it's all right?' she queried, looking at Julia and Ginny.

'Go and enjoy yourselves! It's only one night,' Ginny pointed out.

'OK then.' Thea smiled brightly for Julia's benefit and tried to look like a woman eager to spend the evening being wined and dined by her loving fiancé.

Max raised his hand from Thea's shoulder. His palm tingled where it had been in contact with her smooth, soft skin. She stood up and he could smell her perfume, already as familiar to him as the scent of his own aftershave. His mind whirling, he struggled to make chit-chat with Julia and Ginny before following Thea into the house.

She had gone upstairs, presumably to pack her overnight bag. Max hesitated on the bottom step and debated if he should go and talk to her. He raked his fingers impatiently through his hair. So much for escaping for a few hours!

Deciding against approaching her, he climbed slowly up the stairs.

It hadn't escaped his notice earlier that Julia had looked as though she had been crying again, and he felt sure one of the reasons she wanted both himself and Thea out of the house was so she could have a married women's heart-to-heart with Ginny.

He walked into the ensuite bathroom in the blue bedroom and turned on the shower. If only Julia would confide in him the way she had always done when she was younger. Now, though, she turned away, telling him the problem was between her and Paul and she had to sort things out on her own.

Changing quickly, Max ran back downstairs to the study to collect the documents he needed to drop into the office. A tap on the door made him turn to find Thea waiting for him with a small overnight bag in her hand.

'I'm ready whenever you are.'

Her fair hair was tied back loosely at the nape of her neck and her eyes had the unhappy expression of a woman expecting martyrdom. She had changed from her shorts and vest into a pretty floral sundress.

Picking up his briefcase, he felt mean for wanting to get away from Stony Gables. None of this was Thea's fault, but the last thing he had expected when he had arrived here was to find himself engaged to a stranger, and, what was worse, discovering he was earth-shatteringly attracted to her.

A Perfect Evening...

An hour later, Thea was prowling cautiously around Max's apartment. The journey from Stony Gables had taken longer than expected and getting snarled up in the late afternoon traffic hadn't improved Max's temper. He had spoken very little on the way into the city, merely pointing out some of the landmarks.

The delay in reaching the huge converted warehouse where his penthouse apartment was situated had meant him literally dropping her off and then rushing straight out again to get to his office before his colleagues went home for the evening. So now she was here on her own.

'Make yourself at home, I'll be back soon,' Max had said as he sprinted out of the door.

The view from the window was

certainly spectacular enough, if you liked urban landscapes, she thought as she slid open the patio door to step out on to the steel balcony which ran along the width of the apartment. A galvanised tub with a dispirited-looking plant made an effort at a touch of greenery. Otherwise the balcony was bare except for a couple of uncomfortable-looking mesh chairs and a matching table.

They had entered the building through a gated courtyard with security codes, and even the building was accessed via a swipe card. Thea shivered despite the warm summer air. It felt, to her, like entering prison.

She turned to look back inside the apartment. The rooms were huge from what she'd seen so far, with stripped wooden floors and exposed brickwork walls. Solid metal beams ran across the high ceilings, adding some architectural interest to the rooms and revealing the building's industrial past.

She could see why Julia hadn't felt it

would be a good place for Emily to stay. The lounge was sparsely furnished in true minimalist style and the kitchen was a triumph of black granite surfaces and gleaming stainless steel. There was nothing homely or personal about the apartment at all, and a small child like Emily wouldn't have much freedom to play.

Thea wondered how long Max would be gone. He hadn't suggested she meet his colleagues on this trip; instead they would wait until the formal dinner party tomorrow night. Perhaps he was ashamed of her. She had seen his disapproval of her sundress when she had tapped on the study door at Stony Gables.

Sighing, she smoothed her hand over the cool granite surface of the kitchen worktop.

It wasn't her fault she didn't dress like Gabby. The smart half of her wardrobe consisted mainly of the practical black or navy trousers she wore for work and a variety of shirts. Her off-duty clothes tended to be cheap and cheerful, designed to lift her spirits, and made a divide between what she thought of as her working life and her personal life.

She frowned at her distorted reflection in the gleaming chrome of Max's space-age kettle. Maybe her dress was a little too short and a little too bright. Glancing around at the monochrome colour palette of Max's apartment, she felt as incongruous as a sunflower on an ash heap.

The sound of a key in the lock announced his return and she turned towards the door which led from the lounge to the square hallway. He paused in the doorway; it was awkward knowing he didn't really want her staying here with him.

Noticing the open patio door, he asked, 'What do you think of the view?'

'It's a bit like looking at an anthill with all those people scurrying around. I didn't realise you were so close to the river though.'

They sounded like two strangers at a

house viewing, she thought.

He loosened his collar, eager to shrug off the formal office-wear which was just too warm on such a hot sticky day. Thea's mouth dried as he undid the top buttons of his shirt and pulled the tie free to drop it carelessly on top of the briefcase he had laid on the angular leather couch.

'Did you get yourself a drink?' Slipping off his shoes, he padded over to the large fridge hidden inside one of the tall kitchen cupboards.

Thea shook her head even though he wasn't looking in her direction. Her pulse was fluttering wildly and all her senses were heightened by his presence. Accompanying Max on this trip was a big mistake.

He glanced at her and wrenched open the fridge door. 'There's beer, beer, or beer,' he announced after surveying the contents.

'Then I guess I'll have beer.' She smiled nervously. 'Is that all that's in there?'

He popped off the top and handed her a small bottle. 'Pretty much. I don't do much cooking and I forgot to tell my housekeeper to stock up.'

'The cornflakes might taste interesting in the morning,' she joked.

Max took a long drink from his bottle.

'Listen, about tonight — I'll take the couch.' He nodded towards the black leather sofa.

Heat crept up her neck and into her cheeks. 'It's OK, I can check into a hotel for the night.'

Max frowned. 'What if Julia found out? Or someone else? It would blow everything. We can't take the risk.' He took another sip from his beer bottle.

'Well, let me take the couch then. I'm shorter than you so I'll probably fit better,' Thea offered, her heart beating so wildly she was sure it was audible.

'If anyone's taking the couch, it'll be me. You're my guest.' Max shot her an 'end of discussion' glance.

'Only because Julia left us with no

choice,' Thea responded. 'But you didn't really want me to come with you, did you?'

He froze, the bottle half-way to his lips. 'Was it that obvious?' he asked.

She couldn't fully read his expression, although it looked as if he was concerned that he might have upset her.

'It's all right, I wasn't offended. I can understand that you need some space after the last few days.' She took a deep breath. 'You need time in your own home. That's why I don't mind taking the couch.'

His brown eyes narrowed. 'I don't see the point of us standing here all evening arguing over who sleeps where,' he said finally. 'It's a big flat and we have to carry on sharing a room at your house — at least until Julia catches her plane.' He shrugged his broad shoulders. 'Anyway, we can talk about it later.'

He drained the last of his beer and stowed the empty bottle in the recycling basket under the counter.

'It's a beautiful evening. Let me show you around a little then we can go and try that restaurant Julia was burbling about.'

She looked at him doubtfully for a moment, her blue eyes shadowed and uncertain. Then she gave him a faint smile.

'OK. I'd like to see more of the city.'

He took her for a walk in the small park near to his apartment. It was busy, with people out walking, mothers pushing strollers, people jogging or rollerblading, and lovers walking hand-in-hand along the leafy pathways. He enjoyed strolling along with Thea. She was good company.

The thought worried him and he was glad when they reached the riverside.

The river was busy with tourist boats chugging up and down the water as they ferried passengers between the landmarks of the city.

'It's amazing to think we were paddling this morning in the stream and the water was so clear. This is so

190

. . . different.' Thea stared out over the dark, murky river at the hustle and bustle and shivered slightly.

'Are you getting cold?'

She shook her head. 'Someone walking over my grave.' She flashed him a smile. 'That's what my father used to say.'

Max's heart clenched, and he instinctively slipped his arm around her shoulders. Thea leaned her head against his shoulder and he smelt the soft floral perfume she always wore.

The combination of the delicate fragrance and the sound of the river water slapping against the bank as the boats passed by stirred a chord buried deep in his psyche. Closing his eyes, his mind slipped back to an earlier time, shortly after leaving school and starting university.

He hadn't thought about Laura for years. He had thought he had successfully erased her from his memory, but now a cold, sick feeling of betrayal swept through him. She had been blonde, like Thea, with wide blue eyes.

What a fool he had been. Max swallowed hard. He had been so young and naïve. It had been loneliness, he realised now, that had made him an easy target for a girl like Laura. He had discovered too late that she was another predator, like his own mother — a woman who deliberately sought out men with wealth and connections and used them to further her own ends.

A well-meaning friend had warned him but he had refused to believe the truth, until Laura herself had spelled it out at Henley regatta when she had left him for a wealthier prospect.

'Max?'

He opened his eyes. Thea was looking up at him, her gaze troubled.

'It's cool here. Let's walk on.' He kept his arm around her slim shoulders and she made no move to escape. It led him to wonder about Thea's motives for agreeing to play along with the phony engagement. Was she another Laura? He knew she was desperate to stay at

Stony Gables, but how desperate? Was she using the undeniable attraction between them to try to make the engagement real?

As they took the path leading away from the river, he dropped his arm from her shoulder and thrust his hands deep into his jacket pockets. Now that he had released the doubt genie from the bottle, he started to replay all of Thea's actions in his mind, questioning her motivation for agreeing to go along with the deception.

★　★　★

Max's emotional withdrawal stung more than the mere physical removal of his arm from her shoulders. Thea wished she knew what went on inside his troubled mind. She had always prided herself on her perceptiveness and her ability to tune in to other people's feelings and emotions, but with Max her gift seemed to have deserted her.

Defiantly she raised her chin and quickened her walking pace a little. The easy, comfortable atmosphere between them was gone and despite the warm evening, the hairs on her arms felt goose-bumpy.

'We should go and see if the restaurant Julia suggested has a table free.' Max's tone was casual and she knew he was simply being polite.

'If you like.' She kept her voice offhand. She didn't feel hungry now.

Resisting the urge to cross her arms in a defensive move, she forced herself to look relaxed as she walked along, but all the while her mind was whirring away, worrying about the evening ahead.

The gates from the park out on to the road were in sight and there were more people around now as the busy city nightlife began to spring into action. Young women in groups, all dressed up for an evening out, passed them by as they emerged on to the street. Thea began to feel uncomfortable. Suppose she wasn't dressed properly for the restaurant Julia had recommended? That would be so embarrassing.

'If you'd rather not to go out for dinner I'd be quite happy with a takeaway instead,' she offered hesitantly.

'We're here now.' Max glanced at her, his sharp eyes assessing her. 'What's the matter?'

'Nothing, it looks lovely.' The restaurant did look nice and it didn't appear to be terribly formal as she had feared.

Max frowned and pushed the door open for her to walk through. The restaurant interior was air conditioned and felt blissfully cool against the warmth of her cheeks.

Thea knew she was hopelessly out of practise at all this. After her father had become ill she hadn't dated, and Jon had never taken her anywhere more exciting than his local bar. The whole business of getting dressed up and heading out for a night at a wine-bar or a restaurant had been left behind, along with her girlfriends, when Jon had entered her life.

Max had a quiet word with the waiter and they were led to a table for two on the far side of the restaurant. Although it was early in the evening, Thea noticed that most of the tables were occupied.

'It seems very popular.'

'The food has been good whenever I've been here before,' Max commented.

As he turned his attention back to the menu, she wondered if he had eaten there with Gabby. Most of the customers appeared to be young couples like themselves. She suppressed a sigh. The big difference was that the other customers were enjoying themselves!

The waiter returned, notepad in hand, and Thea realised she hadn't even looked at the menu.

'What would you like?' Max asked.

'Oh, I'm still deciding, you go first.' Already, she felt, she was making an idiot of herself and they hadn't even got to the starters yet.

Max gave his order.

'I'll have the same.' Thea closed her menu and handed it back to the waiter. She didn't have a clue what she had just asked for, but since she liked most Italian food, she figured it didn't really matter. She was too tense to eat any of it anyway.

All these couples looking so happy in each other's company; how did she and Max appear to them? Her engagement ring glittered in the lamplight and guilt settled like cement in her stomach.

'So, what shall we talk about? And don't say you choose!' He smiled at her and Thea guessed he was trying to make amends for whatever it was that had triggered his change of mood by the river.

She fiddled restlessly with the knife nearest to her side plate. 'Tell me about your work. Ginny says your company has diversified into lots of different fields since she stopped working for you?'

The waiter reappeared and uncorked a bottle of wine, leaving it to breathe on the table before moving away.

'I don't know that you'll find it very interesting, but basically we specialise in hunting out investment opportunities. Property development, rentals, failing companies, that kind of thing. I head a small team; they're the people Julia has invited to dinner tomorrow along with their partners.' He leaned back in his chair. 'Your turn now, tell me about your job.'

She smiled faintly. 'It's not as exciting as yours. Before Dad became ill I was teaching at a nursery school. I'd worked my way up to be deputy head of the unit. The job I'm due to start in September is a teaching post at the nursery in town. It's funded by a children's charity so it should be interesting.'

'Isn't it a bit of a climb-down career wise?'

Thea could feel his dark eyes scrutinising her face.

'I suppose so, but I love teaching and, as Tom told you, I don't drive. There aren't that many jobs available that I could apply for. I was lucky this one came up.'

'But if you sold Stony Gables and moved nearer to the city . . .'

The wine waiter reappeared to pour the wine, and Thea waited until he had moved away before she answered.

'I like living at Stony Gables, it's my home. And my new job sounds really interesting. I'm sure I'll learn a lot from it.' She bit her lip, aware that she sounded very defensive.

'I know how much your home means to you,' he acknowledged, picking up on her tone. 'I'm sorry, I was just curious. You didn't want to return where you were working before your father's illness?'

He took a sip of his wine as she explained.

'I had to give up the job: Dad was ill for over twelve months so they couldn't keep the post open. My flat was rented, so there was nothing to go back to.' In spite of her efforts, she heard the wobble in her voice.

Fortunately the first course arrived, giving her time to regain her composure before Max could ask another question. She had thought she had stopped being so sensitive about her past.

Max watched Thea's expressive features covertly as they began the meal. He was certain from her reactions that she had something to hide, but what?

He decided to turn the conversation on to more neutral ground; perhaps if she relaxed a little more he might manage to find out her motivations for agreeing to the fake engagement.

'You and your father must have been very close?' he suggested.

'We were.' She smiled wistfully. 'Mum died when I was fourteen, so it was just me and Dad after that. I suppose it's a similar thing for you and Julia.'

Max considered. 'I hadn't thought of it like that, but yes, you're right.' To all intents and purposes he had been more of a father figure to Julia than a brother; he had always been the one she turned to when she had problems. Except the problems she was experiencing now.

Julia had certainly appeared very anxious for Thea to accompany him on his trip back to the flat. He wondered what she had been discussing with Ginny when he and Thea had returned from the picnic.

He sighed heavily and put his cutlery down.

'Emily seems happier now she knows she's staying with us,' he commented.

Thea was sipping her wine and viewing him cautiously over the rim of the glass, her blue eyes dark and mysterious in the lamplight.

'We just have to keep this charade going till the day after tomorrow when Julia gets on her plane,' he added, and the sinking feeling in the pit of his stomach at the thought that the fake engagement was almost at an end took him by surprise.

Thea frowned. 'We'll have to pretend for a little longer than that or Emily will be upset, although I'm sure we can relax a little. I just hope Julia works her problems out while she's away.'

The waiter reappeared to collect the plates.

'I hope so too. Paul's a nice guy and up till the last few months I thought they were very happy together. Emily adores him.'

The main course arrived and Max took the opportunity to top up their wine glasses.

'Whoa, I'm not used to much alcohol,' Thea warned him as he added more to her glass.

'From what Henry was saying, Stony Gables needs a lot of money spent on it. I'd noticed a few problems,' Max commented.

Thea sighed. 'Repairs to the roof, the guttering, plumbing and heating and redecoration, and that's just the tip of the iceberg. Henry's been pressuring me to turn the house into luxury apartments or sell it to a developer.' She pulled a face. 'There's no way I'd let them pull it down to build those ugly executive box-houses.'

Max struggled to hide a smile as he considered Stony Gables' distinctly unlovely appearance.

'I suppose my renting the house will help solve some of those problems,' he commented. So Thea had been telling the truth about money being her prime motivation for helping him. He was annoyed with himself for feeling disappointed.

Thea nodded enthusiastically. 'Mmm. At least the more urgent stuff like the roof and the heating can be fixed before winter.'

Sitting and chatting with Max in the intimate atmosphere of the restaurant, Thea began to relax as they swapped stories and jokes. Whatever had caused his bad mood earlier appeared to have gone and she started to feel as if she were beginning to understand him a little better.

Sipping her coffee at the end of the meal she became aware that the restaurant had gradually emptied and they were one of the last couples remaining. Her attention had been so focused on the charismatic man masquerading as her fiancé, she hadn't even noticed the other people leaving.

'We should go. I think the waiters would like to go home!' Thea replaced the white china cup carefully on the saucer. Her head had a slightly woozy feel from a little too much alcohol.

Max looked around. He appeared as unaware of the late hour as Thea.

'You're right, we should leave. Julia has our engagement dinner planned for tomorrow and we'll be snoring in the soup at this rate.' He grinned mischievously. It lit up his face and made her heart thump in her chest.

He called the waiter over and settled the bill, brushing aside with a frown Thea's offer to split the costs.

The summer night air was still warm as they left the restaurant and set off on the short walk back to the apartment block.

'It's been a lovely evening.' Thea sighed.

Perhaps it was the alcohol but she felt as if she were floating rather than walking down the street. Max had draped his arm around her shoulders and the gesture felt as comfortable as an old shoe. It was almost as if they were a real couple making their way home after a romantic evening out.

As Max tapped the security code into the lock at the entrance of the complex Thea leaned contentedly against the wall. The smooth, hard surface of the brickwork was reassuringly cool against the heated surface of her skin. The release buzzer sounded and she followed him into the large open communal hall. Their footsteps echoed, bouncing off the stone-flagged floor as they made their way to the lift.

Max kept his fingers loosely linked

with hers as if afraid that breaking contact would break the mood. The lift slid smoothly to a halt on the top floor. Fitting the key into the lock, Max opened the front door of the apartment and stood back to let her go in.

'Would you like another coffee?' He dropped his keys on to the worktop in the kitchen area and turned towards her.

'That would be lovely, thanks.' She didn't really want one, but it delayed the moment when inevitably they would have to get changed and go to their respective beds.

'Max, I really don't mind taking the settee tonight.'

He paused, the coffee spoon suspended over the mug. 'I understand you're nervous because we're alone but I assure I'm not about to pounce on you. I was only teasing earlier.'

Heat rushed into her cheeks. 'I'm sorry, you're right. It's just that everything's been happening so fast.'

He put down the spoon and reached

across, touching her hot cheek with the tip of his finger. 'I know.'

Thea could only stare into his dark eyes, trying to read the confusing mix of emotions showing there.

'I thought I could cope with this fake engagement thing but . . . ' She tried to put her feelings into words but how could she explain?

'You've changed your mind?' Max asked incredulously.

'No, I gave you my word and I wouldn't do anything that might change Julia's mind about letting Emily stay.'

'Then what?'

His question hung in the air between them, both of them knowing instinctively what the problem was but neither of them willing to put their feelings into words.

The silence seemed to stretch for ever. Max waited for Thea to go first. He wasn't sure he could explain what was going on between them. He wasn't sure if he even wanted to. Already in the few days since he had met her his whole world had shifted. Everything he had thought he had decided about his life, his feelings, and his future had been turned upside down.

'I'm not sure that I know how to say this, and I might be about to make a real fool of myself . . . but . . . you and I want different things from life and I know this engagement is only for Julia's benefit but, well . . . ' Her voice tailed off and she flapped her hands desperately.

'But you're attracted to me and I'm attracted to you, is that what you're trying to say?' He scanned her expression for any trace of a mercenary motive and despised himself for doing so.

Relief flooded across her face, her eyes shining like sapphires against the pallor of her skin.

'Exactly! And it's no good.'

Her logic left him floundering for a moment. 'Why?'

She sighed heavily. 'Like I said, we

want different things from life. You told me you aren't planning marriage, a family or commitment of any kind, and I . . . '

'You want those things,' he said flatly. He understood there was a monumental chasm between them over what they each wanted for their futures. 'That doesn't alter the fact that I want you and you want me. We can't control who we're attracted to Thea.'

Her face paled even further and he knew before she spoke that he'd managed to say the wrong thing again.

'Maybe not, but we can control what we do about it.' Her voice sounded stiff.

He raked his hand through his hair and tried to work out what he'd said that had caused her to look so upset.

'You think I'm taking advantage of the situation?'

'Yes. I mean no. Oh, I don't know.' She folded her arms defensively. 'I just think that being together in such close proximity isn't good for either of us. Julia leaves soon, and I think we should cool things a little when she's not around.'

'I see.' He did see. What he didn't understand was why he was so irritated by her suggestion. Wasn't that why he'd tried to come back to his apartment, leaving Thea behind at Stony Gables? To put some space between them and give himself a chance to breathe?

★   ★   ★

He picked up the kettle which had come to the boil and finished making the coffee. Thea had crossed over to the big windows and was leaning against the open glass door looking out across the water at the city lights. He wished he could interpret the expression on her face.

Picking up a mug he carried it across to her, and she seemed to sense his approach without turning. 'You think I'm crazy for wanting a family.' Her voice sounded sad.

He paused, her mug still in his hand.

'No, not crazy.' He hesitated, trying to find the right words. 'You're young yet. I suppose I don't understand the rush. Why you don't have some fun first. You choose to live in that huge house which takes all your time and money and bury yourself away.'

Thea rubbed at the bare flesh at the top of her arms as if the night air had suddenly gone cold.

'I don't expect you to understand, but I love my life, I love my home. I have a close circle of friends who I can rely on, and although I'll never be rich from my work, I enjoy it. I just don't have a family.'

She half turned to face him and he automatically proffered her the coffee mug. She accepted it almost without noticing.

'I'm not scared of being alone, I just want the normal things in life — a partner who loves me and who I love. A family life with children. Before Dad became ill I thought I'd found that person.' She paused, struggling with her emotions. 'It turned out he couldn't control who he fell in love with either.' Tears spilled down her cheeks and she dashed them away with her free hand. 'I'm sorry.'

Max rescued the mug from her trembling fingers and set it down on the nearby coffee table. He longed to take her in his arms and wipe away the sadness from her face.

'Were you engaged?' A surge of jealousy speared him at the thought of this unknown man breaking Thea's heart.

She shook her head. 'We'd talked about getting married, made plans together for finding a house. Then when Dad became ill and it was obvious he couldn't go on living on his own, I moved back home to care for him. Jon phoned and visited a lot at first, but then as time went on he — well, he found someone else. I was the last person to find out.' She fumbled in her pocket for a tissue and scrubbed at her eyes. 'I felt so stupid.'

'No wonder this is so hard on you. I take it you don't see this guy Jon any more?' If he ever met this guy he didn't think he would be responsible for the consequences. He passed her a clean folded handkerchief from his pocket.

'He married the other girl.'

A jumble of conflicting emotions whirled around in Max's mind. A dark surge of jealousy demanded an answer. 'Are you still in love with him?'

'I don't think that's any of your business.' She gave her eyes another fierce dab with the handkerchief, then picked up her coffee and held it defensively in front of her like a shield, clearly regretting having told him so much about her past.

'What about you, Max? Have you ever been in love?'

She waited for his answer. She wasn't sure where she'd found the courage to ask the question, but her pride demanded an answer.

'I thought I was once.' He was looking past her, staring out at the night-time cityscape.

'What happened?' Instinctively she knew it was important, another tiny clue to the enigma of his complex personality.

'It turned out she loved money more than me. A richer prospect came along and she took off.' He shrugged. 'It was a long time ago.' His expression closed and became more guarded. She sensed he wasn't prepared to share any more of his past with her tonight.

'Go to bed, Thea. I've got some work I need to finish off.'

She was being dismissed. Anger flooded through her; the sharing of confidences was clearly only going to flow one way. He plainly intended to bury himself in the spare room which was fitted out with every piece of office equipment known to man.

Drawing a deep breath to steady herself, she placed her mug carefully on the table.

'Goodnight, Max.'

He didn't answer, seemingly unaware

of her presence as he stared out at the night sky. Thea took herself and her battered pride off to bed.

Closing the bedroom door quietly behind her she leaned against it and tried to calm her racing heart. It was hopeless. He had made his position clear and he wasn't about to compromise, though for a moment out there she had thought he was about to share with her, to open up a little and begin to expose some of the emotions and feelings he kept buried deep within his heart. She wondered if he would ever manage to deal with the emotional baggage he carried.

Slipping off her sandals she walked over to the bed, the polished wooden floorboards cool under the soles of her feet. She sank down on to the soft blue duvet.

It had sounded as though Max planned to stay in his office and work for as long as possible. Hiding from his emotions, she decided impatiently.

Shaking off the thought, she grabbed

her night clothes and stomped into the shower room. One thing she wasn't, she thought as she brushed her teeth, she wasn't a quitter.

The optimistic side of her nature bubbled back to the fore and as she changed into her pyjamas she decided there was no point in worrying about things she had little control over. It wasn't as if she could force Max into discussing the issues which coloured his feelings about women and relationships.

Uneasily she shrugged off the doubts which still niggled at the corners of her mind. She had given her word that she would help him care for his little niece. Julia would be gone soon and Emily's welfare was what was really important, not some stupid infatuation she had for the child's uncle. At the end of the day Max was her employer and maybe she should try keeping that more in mind in future.

Lying alone in the vast expanse of Max's double bed Thea thought she would never manage to fall asleep. Every nerve was on the alert. She underestimated her tiredness, however, and she had long since fallen asleep before Max finally switched off his computer and made up his bed on the far-from-comfortable sofa in the lounge.

'Our Feelings Won't
Go Away'

Coffee, she could smell coffee. Opening her eyes she looked around and recalled where she was.

There was a light tap on the bedroom door, and Thea instinctively pulled the covers a little higher as she struggled to sit up.

'Come in.'

Max was carrying a tray with a mug and a plate of biscuits.

'Sorry, there's no toast. I forgot we hadn't any bread.'

Her heart was thumping as she accepted the tray. Staring up at him she noticed the dark circles under his eyes and wondered how late it had been before he had gone to sleep.

'Thea, I've been thinking about last night, about what you said.' He had his hands stuffed in the pockets of his jeans and he appeared ill at ease. She waited anxiously for him to explain. Was he calling off the engagement?

The palms of her hands grew sweaty with anxiety at the thought, and she scolded herself mentally for being so foolish after the pep talk she had given herself last night.

'I feel I owe you an apology. I won't pretend that I'm not attracted to you, you know I am. But I realised after our conversation last night that we need to be more circumspect and practical about our arrangement.'

She listened to his extraordinary speech with a growing sense of anger and bewilderment. She stifled the little voice in her head that told her she should be pleased he was taking this line. After all, wasn't it only what she herself had suggested?

He cleared his throat, clearly waiting for her response.

Slowly and with deliberate care she slid the tray to one side, annoyance at his easy dismissal of his feelings overriding what, she belatedly realised, after she'd opened her mouth, was her common sense.

'Circumspect! Max, you're not addressing a board meeting! You and I are not the proposed merger of two business interests!'

He took a step back as she slid out of bed, hands on hips to confront him.

'I did a lot of thinking last night too, and I realised something. OK, I agree we need to separate our feelings from the task of caring for Emily and reassuring Julia.' She poked him in the chest with her forefinger. 'But the feelings we have for one another won't just go away. You know, the real difference betweenus isn't in the way we see our futures. It's in the way we see ourselves.'

Waving his hands in a placating motion he stepped back again, attempting to avoid her accusatory finger. But it was useless.

'Yes, I want marriage and a family,

but I'm willing to be open to new relationships. I might have had one really bad experience, but that doesn't mean I judge everyone else the same way. When are you going to be prepared to do that? To share the real you with someone?'

'So what are you saying? That I'm afraid to have a relationship?' The words sounded like a growl and his dark eyes glittered dangerously.

Lifting her chin, Thea stared him down. 'Well, aren't you?'

'No!' He glowered back at her.

'Prove it!'

'What?' Her demand had clearly taken him by surprise. She could see the pulse throbbing in his temple, and for a moment she held her breath, wondering if she had pushed him too far.

His eyes locked with hers, then, to her surprise, he started to laugh.

'OK, Miss Smarty-pants, and how do I do that?'

'When did you last take a risk? Take a

chance? And I don't mean work-wise,' she said quickly when he would have opened his mouth and interrupted her. 'I mean emotionally. When did you last fight for a relationship?'

His dark eyes narrowed and he shot her a hostile glance. Tension hung in the air and Thea's jaw hurt from clenching her teeth so hard.

'This is ridiculous!' He turned on his heel and stalked out, and a moment later the apartment door slammed shut behind him.

'Infuriating, bossy, know-all schoolteacher!' he muttered as he headed down the stairs, spurning the lift in an attempt to vent his feelings with exercise. When had he last taken a risk? The day he had first met Thea and got himself embroiled in this crazy deception, that was when. But she made it sound as if he was some kind of emotional cripple!

He paused on the bottom step and ran his hand through his hair in exasperation. What was he doing? In the space of a few days Thea had turned his nice orderly existence on its head.

He slumped against the cool exposed brickwork of the stairwell. But they had no choice but to see this farce through to the end.

He closed his eyes and drew in a deep breath. At least one thing had come out of his argument with Thea. She had been forthright about wanting marriage and a family and equally frank that she didn't view him as a candidate. Good, he told himself firmly, at least that was one less problem to worry about. Wasn't it?

* * *

The journey back to Stony Gables was silent except for the music on the car radio. Thea kept her attention fixed firmly on the passing scenery.

Max hadn't said much after his return to the apartment. She knew he had been to the gym which was situated within the complex as he had returned carrying a bag of sports gear which he had dumped into the washing machine before going into his bedroom and packing a small case of clothes to take down to Stony Gables.

The grey concrete of the motorway scenery was rapidly giving way to the greener fields and hedgerows which brought them closer to home with each mile that passed. Thea's stomach started to feel uncomfortable as she pictured Emily and Julia's trusting faces waiting for them. There was no way that she and Max were good enough actors to convince them that they had had a blissful time, alone in each other's company. The icily polite silence was a bit of a giveaway, not to mention the body language. Or lack of it.

Max swung the car in through the gates of Stony Gables and slid to a halt on the gravel outside the house. The comforting sight of the stone gargoyles which guarded her front door boosted her spirits.

She glanced across at Max as he

switched off the engine. For a moment he paused, as if steeling himself for the task ahead. Thea's heart gave an inconvenient twinge of sympathy.

The front door was flung open and Emily came bouncing down the steps, her small face beaming with delight at their return.

'Uncle Max, look at my new dress!' Without waiting for them to get out of the car, she started twirling around in the sunshine. Thea opened the door and climbed out.

Emily paused in her twirling and grinned happily at her. 'Do you like my dress, Aunty Thea? Mummy bought it for me 'cos she says I can't go to the big party tonight.'

'I think it's really lovely, Emily. You look like a princess.'

Emily smiled and hugged her with a fierceness which took Thea by surprise.

'Do I get a hug, too?' Max had climbed out of the car and was standing watching them with a thoughtful expression on his face.

Emily released her grip on Thea and rushed across to him with a whoop of delight, and as she watched them embrace Thea wished she could get Max to understand about families. It was plain to see how much he loved Emily; he'd even been prepared to pretend to be engaged, for heaven's sake!

Sighing, she turned away towards the open front door. Her interference so far hadn't done much good. If anything she'd made things worse instead of better.

Julia was sitting in the kitchen. 'I thought I heard the car. Emily couldn't wait for you both to get back.' She stood up and went to the fridge. 'I put a jug of juice in the fridge earlier; I thought you'd like a drink when you got back.'

'That was kind of you, Julia. Thank you.' Thea was touched by her thoughtfulness.

Max's sister, although still pale, looked better than she had done on her arrival at Stony Gables.

'I can't tell you what a relief it is to know Emily will be so happy and contented here with you and Max while I'm away.' Julia reached into the fridge for the jug of juice and poured some into a tall glass. 'I must admit when Max first suggested looking after Emily I really didn't think it was going to work out, but since I've met you and seen how at home she is here, I can see it's the right choice.'

Thea forced herself to smile as she accepted the glass of juice while guilt about the extent of hers and Max's deception settled in her stomach like a lead weight.

'Everyone's coming tonight. Ginny and Laurence and Max's partners and their wives. It should be a really nice evening. I called in to the restaurant this morning with Emily when we bought her new dress and it's a very attractive venue.'

Julia slid the jug back into the fridge and came and sat down opposite Thea with her own drink. 'Emily has dragged Max down the garden to push her on the swing.'

Thea quashed a tiny feeling of relief and forced herself to relax.

'You must be looking forward to seeing Paul again.'

Julia sipped her drink thoughtfully. 'I am now. I've had time to think things through and the last few times I've spoken to him on the phone I get the feeling that he's been doing some thinking too, so I feel much more hopeful than I have for a long time.'

Impulsively Thea reached across to squeeze her hand. 'I'm so glad.'

'I'm pleased Max met you,' Julia said warmly. 'Have you given any thought to a date for the wedding yet?'

Thea wriggled uncomfortably. 'We haven't really discussed it. I mean, there's no reason to rush into anything.'

'The vicar was asking Ginny if you'd set a date. I must say I think your village church looks like a very pretty setting for a wedding.'

Thea had always pictured herself marrying at the lovely old parish church. A tantalising vision flashed through her mind of white lace and a horse-drawn carriage decked with flowers with a smiling groom who looked suspiciously like Max standing next to the open carriage door.

She was unaware that she had drifted off into a daydream till she heard Julia's voice speaking to someone.

'Has Emily let you escape? Sit down and I'll get you a drink. It's thirsty work pushing her on the swing.'

Max pulled out the empty chair next to Thea and sat down. His arm brushed hers, and a tingle swept through her.

'Emily's still outside. I think she's planning on doing some watering,' he informed his sister.

'Oh, no! Not in her new dress!' Julia dashed outside.

'You two seemed deep in conversation.' Max poured himself a drink from the jug Julia had left on the table.

'Apparently the vicar's been asking

Ginny if we've set a date yet.'

She braced herself for his reaction, but much to her surprise he didn't appear as mortified as she had expected.

'I expect we'll get a lot more comments like that, and worse, at dinner tonight.' He took a sip of juice. 'What did you tell her?'

'The truth. That it's something we haven't discussed yet.'

She thought his shoulders relaxed a little at her answer. The tension which had hung in the air between them all the way back had lessened slightly and Thea hoped the atmosphere was improving, otherwise the dinner party was going to be the challenge to end all challenges.

Max set his glass on the table. 'I'd better go and get some work done. I promised Emily I would take her down by the river later.'

The speed with which he excused himself and the way he didn't quite meet her eyes as he left made her suspect he was using work as an escape from her company.

'Oh, get over yourself,' she muttered. All she had to do was get through this dinner party and wave Julia off on her flight tomorrow. She bit down the urge to cry. Who was she kidding — 'all she had to do'? It would have been hard enough to pull off if she and Max had still been in tune. Now, with this frostiness between them, it would be so much more difficult, as if the differences in their lifestyles weren't enough.

The dinner party people would all be expecting someone like Gabby, too, she thought gloomily, poised and sophisticated. It was no use, she thought, glancing down at her usual T-shirt and jeans — she needed help.

The Engagement Party

'Thea! What on earth — ?' Ginny opened the front door wider and reached out a hand to pull her inside.

The worried expression on Ginny's face confirmed Thea's suspicion that she must look a complete mess. The tears had started to flow as she had cycled along the lane.

'Come through to the conservatory. Whatever's the matter?'

Thea allowed Ginny to steer her through to one of the comfortable sofas in the sun lounge. Sniffing miserably, she wiped her eyes on the remains of a tissue from her pocket.

'I can't do this any more. Oh, Ginny, you were right! This whole thing has been the most awful mistake.'

'What's happened?' Ginny asked, passing her a box of tissues.

Thea sniffed and sobbed her way

through her sad tale, then waited for Ginny's verdict on what she should do.

'I'm not going to be able to carry this off tonight, Ginny. They'll be expecting someone like Gabby and instead they'll get me and . . . '

' . . . and now that you're in love with Max it hurts to go on pretending that you have a future together.' Ginny finished the sentence for her, leaving Thea gaping open-mouthed.

'I feel partly responsible for all this,' Ginny went on. 'I would never have suggested Max rent your house if I'd thought the two of you . . . ' She sighed. 'But Max has always been so anti-marriage, and you've never wanted the kind of man who didn't share your goals.'

Thea was shaking her head. 'None of this is your fault. It's not as if *you're* the one who came up with the idea of faking the engagement.'

'No, but I couldn't resist a spot of matchmaking by sending you off to Max's apartment with him when Tom said you two had been kissing. I'm sorry — I shouldn't have interfered.'

'No, Ginny. You warned me right at the start what Max is like. I guess I just got swept along by my feelings into imagining that I could change him. But how am I going to get through tonight?'

'That depends on what you want to achieve. If you're asking me to help you look like the kind of woman Max's business partners are expecting to meet, then that's no problem.' Ginny paused. 'If you want advice on Max, then I don't think I'll be much help. To me he looks like a man who's head over heels in love with you when he's around you, but you say that isn't the case . . . '

Thea pulled a face. Max might be attracted to her but he had been quite clear about not being in love.

'I'll settle for looking more like the kind of woman he would get engaged to.' At least I'll keep my dignity and I can retain some pride, she thought.

Ginny gave her a comforting hug. 'Let's go and see what we can find in my wardrobe then. There are some lovely things from my 'pre-Tom' days which should fit you.' She gave Thea's hand a pat. '*I'll* never fit in them again, that's for certain!'

★ ★ ★

Thea's bike was missing from by the back door. Max noticed it had gone as soon as he and Emily neared the house as they returned from their riverside walk.

'I'm going to show Mummy my caterpillar.' Emily danced off with the jam jar full of leaves and the somnolent looking caterpillar he had persuaded her to take when they had failed in their attempts to catch anything in the stream.

Aimlessly he wandered back outside and around to the front of the house. Thea had been right about the amount of work the house needed. He squinted up at the gutters. Most of them were still the original cast iron and were long past their life span. The paint was peeling from the window ledges and some of the sills were rotten.

The sound of Thea's squeaky old bike at the bottom of the drive drew his attention away from his mental list of Stony Gables' faults. Much to his annoyance Thea wasn't alone. Crawling alongside her with the window rolled down was a familiar sports car. Henry!

They were deep in conversation as Max neared the car. The wicker basket of Thea's bike was full of carrier bags, and she had dismounted to talk to Henry. Her hair was blowing around her face in the light, late afternoon breeze and her cheeks were flushed from exertion.

'Thea — Henry.' Thea hadn't noticed him approaching but at the sound of his greeting she turned round. 'Let me take your bike for you, darling.' Max emphasised the last word causing Thea to flush a deeper shade of pink as he took firm possession of the handlebars of the bike.

'Max. Didn't realise you were still here. Congratulations, by the way — I heard about the engagement.' Henry leered at Thea. 'You've got quite a catch here, old boy. Well, I'd best be off. See you around, Thea.' With a brief nod Henry slipped the car into gear and roared away.

'What did he want?' Max demanded. Ever since he had met Henry at Ginny's house, he had disliked and distrusted him.

Thea had fallen into step beside him as he pushed her ancient bike up the driveway. 'He was just being pleasant for once.'

The scoffing sound which escaped his lips slipped out automatically, bringing a furrow to Thea's brow. She reached across and took the carrier bag from the bicycle basket.

'Thanks for wheeling the bike up. If you'll excuse me, I've a lot to do to get ready for tonight.'

Her voice was stiff and he sensed he had done the wrong thing yet again. As he watched her walk away with her chin held defiantly in the air, he suppressed a growl of frustration.

Wheeling the bike back into its usual position outside the back door, his imagination was whirling around at the same speed as the bike wheels. Bitterly he forced himself to face facts. It had been jealousy, pure and simple, which had driven him to storm down the driveway and intervene in Thea and Henry's conversation.

He didn't like feeling that things were sliding out of his control. He had prided himself for so many years on his mastery of his emotions and the raw rush of annoyance had taken him completely by surprise.

Thea tipped the contents of the carrier bags out on her bed. Picking up the dress which Ginny had loaned her for the evening, she slipped it on to a hanger and hooked it carefully on to her wardrobe door.

The heart-to-heart talk with Ginny had helped clarify things in her mind, and knowing she had her friend's support, the evening ahead seemed a little less daunting.

Running into Max on the driveway had shaken her confidence a little. It was typical of her luck that Henry had rolled up just as she had arrived home. Her hands shook a little as she sorted out the toiletries and cosmetics she had picked up in the village on the way home.

She could hear Julia talking to Emily in the tower bedroom. Ginny had arranged for Emily to stay at her house for the night with Tom while the adults went out to celebrate the engagement. Emily was excited about the prospect of a sleepover and had hatched a good many plans with Tom which they had discussed in noisy whispers and lots of giggles.

Thea sank down despondently on to her bed. She had never envisaged life becoming this complicated when she had agreed to faking an engagement to Max. In the short space of time Emily had been in the house she had become very fond of the little girl, and Emily had become fond of her. What was going to happen later when Thea and Max made their announcement that the engagement was off?

Flopping back, Thea lay on top of her quilt and closed her eyes, allowing the familiar sounds of the house to wash over her. Julia was leaving in the morning, then it was down to Thea and Max to ensure that Emily had a happy and fun-filled stay.

'Focus, Thea,' she told herself sternly. 'You're doing this for Emily.'

She wondered what Max's colleagues would be like. Julia had told her a little about them and Max had filled her in on some details, too. Even so, she had an uneasy feeling that she wasn't going to be the kind of woman they would have expected Max to propose to — although from what Max himself and everyone else had said, they would be astonished that he had proposed to anyone at all!

By the time she had showered, carefully applied her make-up and changed into the beautiful pale blue dress that Ginny had loaned her, butterflies were dancing nervously in her stomach. Using the potions she had acquired from the chemist she tamed her hair into a smooth neat chignon, and by the time she surveyed the final result in the mildew-spotted mirror on her wardrobe door, she hardly recognised herself.

'Very corporate wife,' she muttered, uncertain that she liked her new image.

A knock at the door disturbed her reverie.

'Come in.'

Max pushed the door open cautiously.

'You look very nice.' He paused as if uncertain of his welcome. 'I wanted to talk to you before we go downstairs.'

She beckoned him into the room. He closed the door behind him.

'I want to thank you for going

through with this, Thea. I never thought everything would become so complicated. Once Julia's gone, hopefully the madness will die down.'

Thea swallowed. She could read the underlying text of what he was saying. In other words, once Julia was gone, they could stop pretending and begin to pave the way to ending the engagement.

'We'll need to spend a lot of time with Emily,' she pointed out. 'She's going to miss Julia terribly. They're very close, and although Emily seems much happier since she's been here, whenever Julia mentions leaving, she goes very quiet.'

'I've booked a week off work so I can be here to take her out and play with her. I thought it might help take her mind off things.'

Thea was touched that he had thought about how Emily was going to cope without her mother. 'I'd thought of taking her to Treetops — you know, the amusement park,' she put in. 'Tom's told her all about the rides and the animals and she really wants to go. It would give her something to look forward to.'

'OK, sounds good, Treetops it is. We'll take her after Julia's gone, it might cheer her up.'

His face still looked grave as if he wanted to say something else. She hadn't realised while they were talking how close he was standing to her, and her pulse was taking on that crazy rhythm again.

'We'd better go downstairs — Julia and Emily will be waiting.'

She picked up her silver evening purse from the bed and waited for Max to open the door. His eyes met hers and for a heartbeat she thought he was going to kiss her. Instead he suddenly turned away and wrenched the door open.

Her heart was pounding as she joined him at the top of the stairs.

'Ready?' he asked. His voice was cool and controlled and his expression held no trace of the feelings she had thought she'd seen a moment earlier.

Unable to trust her voice she nodded and placed her hand in his, and together they walked down the broad oak staircase into the hall where Julia and Emily were waiting, Emily clutching her overnight bag.

'Wow! Thea, you look beautiful,' Emily squealed.

Julia stepped forward to hug Thea in a gentle embrace. 'You look lovely.' Her dark eyes, so like those of her brother and her daughter, looked wistful for a moment, then she smiled and said, 'We'd better set off or Tom will have expired with anticipation before we get there.'

Tom was standing by the front door when they pulled into Ginny's drive. 'They're here! Mum, Emily's here!' They could hear him shouting to his parents before they were out of the car.

Laurence came out to meet them and Tom and Emily ran into the house with Tom talking excitedly to Emily as he carried her bag.

'Ginny's just finishing getting ready,' Laurence explained. 'Come through to the conservatory. We've time for a drink before we go to meet the others at the restaurant.'

The conservatory was pleasantly cool with the ceiling fans whirring gently and the blinds half drawn to provide some shade from the evening sun. Laurence poured out glasses of Pimms, though since Julia had volunteered to drive he handed her a glass of juice.

Ginny walked in, still fastening a long gold earring on to her ear. 'The babysitter has just arrived so she's gone in to the children.'

Laurence handed her a glass of juice.

'Aren't you drinking?' Thea was surprised; Ginny was very fond of Pimms.

Flushing prettily, Ginny took a seat on the sofa next to Julia.

Laurence cleared his throat. 'This seems as good a time as any for our announcement — Ginny and I are expecting a brother or sister for Tom.'

'Oh, that's fantastic!' Thea hugged

her friend with delight and kissed Laurence on the cheek. Julia and Max joined in with the congratulations, although from Julia's reaction Thea suspected that Ginny may have already told her the news.

Thea couldn't help feeling envious as she watched Laurence beam with pride at his wife. If anything she now felt even guiltier about deceiving Julia and Max's colleagues.

Max seemed to sense her disquiet and once they had finished their drinks and were walking out to the car he came over to walk with her. Allowing the others to get a little ahead of them he slipped his arm around her and murmured in her ear, 'I know you feel bad about this, Thea, but I promise that we'll sort everything out as soon as possible. Just remember, we're doing this for all the right reasons.'

'You're right. I just wish we'd thought it through a little better. Maybe winging it wasn't such a great plan after all.'

As he handed her into Julia's car, he gave her fingers a sympathetic squeeze.

★　★　★

The Limes bistro was housed in an elegant Georgian building which had once been a coaching inn. Now the inside had been stripped back and the beautiful architectural features of the building glowed in the subdued lighting.

'This looks wonderful,' Ginny remarked approvingly. 'It was so rundown before.'

The head waiter recognised Julia and came to greet them with the news that the rest of the party had arrived and were already seated waiting for them. Thea was acutely aware of the interest her arrival was creating as they approached the table. The wives of Max's colleagues all seemed very friendly although openly curious about her. To her relief none of them appeared to be as polished or superior as Gabby.

Julia performed the introductions and Max was soon the subject of much ribaldry from his friends about his surrendering of his eligible-bachelor status.

'Well, Max, I must admit we never thought you'd succumb and join the ranks of the old marrieds like us.' One of his colleagues thumped Max heartily on the back then winked at Thea. 'Still, you certainly picked a beauty.'

Thea could feel her cheeks burning with embarrassment.

The evening was exhausting. The other women were naturally full of questions about how they had met and when they were planning on getting married, was Max selling his flat, and all kinds of things for which Thea had no definite answers. Most of them she could parry with, 'We haven't decided yet,' or, 'Everything's happened so fast,' but the strain of trying not to compound their original deception with further lies was tiring and she was glad when the meal was finished and they were drinking their coffees. The end was in sight!

The restaurant was quieter now and the waiters were clearing some of the tables when Thea heard a familiar voice behind her.

'Thea! You didn't say you were eating here tonight.'

Her heart sank. Turning, she saw Henry, swaying slightly on his heels, accompanied by Gabby. An awkward silence fell. It was clear that everyone knew Gabby and were wondering if Thea knew about her too.

'Gabby — Henry.' Max acknowledged them with a terse nod of his head.

'Well, this is quite a gathering. Is it for anything special?' Gabby directed her question to Max, ignoring Thea completely as if she had never met her before.

'We're celebrating Max and Thea's engagement,' Julia remarked coolly, her tone betraying the fact that she had no affection for Max's ex-girlfriend.

'Ah, yes, silly me, I'd forgotten about that.' Gabby's voice was dismissive and faintly scornful.

Henry leered at Thea. 'I hardly recognised you at first, Thea, all scrubbed up like that. It makes a change from your chicken-cleaning clothes.'

Thea willed the polished elm-wood boards beneath her feet to open up and swallow her.

'Fortunately for me, I'd say Thea looks beautiful whatever she's wearing.' Max glared at Henry as if daring him to take another shot at Thea.

'Come on, Henry, we must get going,' Gabby put in smoothly. 'Good-bye, Max — Julia — erm, thingy.' She waggled her fingers dismissively at Thea then, linking arms with Henry, they left.

Everyone at the table watched them go in stunned silence then broke out into inconsequential chatter in order to cover the awkwardness of the moment.

Julia reached across the table to give Thea's arm a reassuring touch. 'I'm sorry about that, Thea. I'm so glad you're going to be my sister-in-law and not that . . . vixen.'

Thea gave her a weak smile. Gabby clearly still had the knives out for her, and she could only wonder what Max had ever seen in the other girl in the first place.

Max was having exactly the same thoughts. The qualities which had first attracted him to Gabby now seemed repellent; the aloofness and lack of emotional attachment which he had prized because it had meant he was in no danger of falling in love now appeared cold and calculating.

He had been sincere when he had defended Thea. Although Thea looked incredibly lovely and polished this evening, he preferred her in the diaphanous floaty dress she had worn to Ginny's with her hair wild and loose around her shoulders.

He shifted uncomfortably in his seat. He had no business preferring Thea in anything! He had to start putting some distance between them if they were to get through the next few weeks and end the fake engagement amicably without Thea getting hurt. Or *you* getting hurt, his subconscious muttered.

They dropped Ginny and Laurence off at their home and Julia peeped in on her sleeping daughter before they headed back to Stony Gables.

As they set off again, Julia said, 'I want to thank both of you for everything you're doing for Emily. I'm telling you now because tomorrow I'm going to be too tearful to make much sense!'

Max glanced at her. Her eyes were bright and he knew she was dreading leaving Emily even though she was anxious to see Paul.

'Julia, you know I'm always here for you both no matter what happens,' Max said, then his eyes met Thea's in the rear-view mirror, uttering an unspoken plea.

'We'll take good care of Emily,' Thea assured her swiftly. 'You'll speak to her on the phone and email her. Then before you know it you'll be back.'

'I know, but I want to let you know how grateful I am to you. You've both made so many sacrifices for us.'

It was a good thing she wasn't aware of the full extent of the sacrifices they'd made, Max thought.

Julia swung the car in between the gateposts which marked the entrance to Stony Gables and parked next to Max's car. Under the harsh yellow of the interior light Max noticed a tear slide down his sister's cheek.

A Lot On His Mind

Thea woke early the next morning, uncertain of what had disturbed her, until she realised Julia was awake and moving around, the squeaky wooden floorboards betraying her movements.

Slipping out of bed, Thea pulled on her old cotton dressing-gown and went downstairs to make a pot of tea. Julia was probably packing the remainder of her things and would no doubt be glad of a cup.

However, as she reached the hall she could hear the kettle whistling. Julia must have been downstairs to put the kettle on already, she decided. Stifling a yawn she pushed open the kitchen door — and was surprised to find Max pouring the boiling water into the teapot.

'Oh! You're up early.' Self-consciously she hugged her dressing-gown more closely around her.

'I heard Julia pottering about so I thought I'd come and make us all some tea. Want one?'

'Thanks. I expect she's finishing her packing.'

'We're picking up her other luggage on the way to the airport,' he told her. He poured out three mugs of tea, his face sobering as if he had just realised the full implications of what he had taken on in agreeing to care for his niece.

'I'll take Julia's tea up to her,' Thea offered. It was strangely intimate standing together in the kitchen like that.

'Thea . . .'

She turned back to see him watching her, stubble dark on his chin and an unreadable expression in his dark eyes.

'What?'

He hesitated, then shrugged. 'Nothing, it's OK. I'll see you later.'

Puzzled, she left him in the kitchen and went upstairs to Julia's room.

'I brought you some tea.'

'That's kind of you. I didn't disturb you, did I?' Julia looked anxious.

'No, not really. I usually get up early to see to the chickens.'

Julia looked relieved. Her overnight bag was open on the bed and she'd clearly been packing the last of her things. A small photograph of a man in a silver frame lay next to the bag.

'Is that Paul?' Thea could see the resemblance to Emily in the shape of his face and the small dimple in his cheek.

Julia nodded and sighed gently as she picked up the picture to place it carefully in her bag.

'He's going to meet me off the plane. We had a long talk the other day, when you and Max were away. I'm really hoping we can work things out. At least we're talking again and not just shouting at each other,' she said, zipping the bag shut.

'You love each other and you both love Emily, so I'm sure you'll manage to sort out your problems,' Thea assured her and gave her a hug.

'Thank you. Knowing Emily will be so happy and well cared for here takes some of the worry away. I hated the idea of her staying with Aunt Nettie, but I didn't know what else to do. That my brother has finally seen sense and settled down is a huge relief.'

Guilt made Thea uncomfortable and she dropped her gaze.

'We'll look after Emily,' she vowed.

Ginny brought Emily home an hour before Julia was due to leave for the airport.

'She's had a great time. I promised her she could sleep over again some other time if you and Max didn't mind,' Ginny said as Emily raced into the house ahead of her.

'It's fine with me, and I'm sure Max won't mind.' Thea led the way to the kitchen and picked up the kettle. 'Have you got time for a cup of tea?'

Ginny pulled a face. 'Tom and Laurence want to go to the banger car races this morning so I have to get straight back. I'll just nip up and say goodbye to Julia, if that's OK, and then I have to dash.'

Ginny passed Max in the kitchen doorway as she headed upstairs.

'I hear Emily's back,' Max said with a grin to Thea. 'She was full of stories about Tom's toys and how many spoons of sugar he puts on his cereal when Ginny isn't looking!'

Thea laughed. 'That sounds like Tom. It's probably done her good staying there last night. Helped take her mind off her mum leaving today.'

Max checked his watch. 'Julia and I will have to leave for the airport soon. Will you be all right with Emily till I get back?'

'We'll be fine,' she assured him. 'I've got some different toys to distract her with if she gets upset but I'm sure she'll be OK.' Her experience with children had taught her that they were usually far more resilient and sensible than the adults around them expected them to be.

'I'll just check the traffic reports,' Max commented, heading to the study.

Thea guessed that he was concerned for his sister as much as for Emily, and left alone in the kitchen she busied herself with preparing her baking things. She planned to make jam tarts with Emily as a means of distracting the little girl from her mother's leaving.

All too soon it was time for Julia to go. After a final hug and kiss from her daughter she climbed reluctantly into the car and Max pulled away. Emily waved till they turned the corner at the bottom of the drive and disappeared from view.

'Are you all right, sweetie?' Thea hunkered down so her face was level with Emily's.

'Will Mummy make my daddy come home?' Emily avoided Thea's gaze and instead concentrated on kicking at a pebble on the driveway.

'I hope so. I'm sure they'll be back before you've even had time to miss them.'

'I don't want Mummy to make Daddy come back if he shouts at Mummy and makes her cry.'

Emily's mouth turned down at the corners and her lower lip started to tremble, and Thea's heart ached for the troubled little girl.

'Your mummy told me only this morning that she and your daddy weren't going to shout at each other any more. And they both love you very much.'

Emily frowned. 'People shouldn't shout at other people if they love them. It's not very nice.'

'No, it's not, but we all do and say things we shouldn't sometimes when we're cross with someone.' Thea squeezed Emily's hands gently. 'Come on, I want us to go and make a special surprise for Uncle Max for when he gets back. Will you help me?'

Emily hesitated for a split second. 'Is it messy?'

'It can be.'

'Oh, goody! Mummy never lets me

do messy things at home.' Her face brightened and she allowed Thea to lead her to the kitchen.

★ ★ ★

By the time Max returned from the airport he was surprised to smell baking in the air and to hear the sounds of giggling from somewhere. His spirits rose at the sound. He had been concerned that Emily might be inconsolable at Julia leaving.

'Anybody home?' he called as he let himself in at the front door.

He walked on through the hall and headed for the kitchen. A tray of jam tarts stood cooling on the worktop, and next to them were three larger tarts all decorated with pastry scraps to resemble faces.

Smiling to himself he continued on through the kitchen and out into the back garden. That was where the laughter seemed to be coming from.

'Thea? Emily!' he called.

A jet of water shot over the top of the raspberry canes, followed by a shriek of laughter as a small swimsuit-clad figure ran across the grass in front of him.

'Watch out, Uncle Max!' Emily cried as she ran past to take refuge behind the sundial.

Another jet of water sprayed over the canes, narrowly missing him and causing Emily to gurgle with delight as he was forced to skip quickly sideways in order to avoid a soaking.

'Thea's got the hosepipe!' Emily called and shrieked as another spray of water found her hiding place.

Thea emerged from behind the raspberry canes. Wearing a shocking pink bikini top and blue shorts, she looked as wet as Emily. It wasn't until she came nearer that Max realised he was looking far too vulnerable and dry. But it was too late for him to escape — Thea blasted him with the hose, soaking his shorts and tee shirt.

Emily was laughing so hard by now she was rolling around on the grass holding her stomach, squealing with delight.

'Just you wait!' Recovering his breath from the coldness of his drenching, Max took a step forward to grab at Thea. But realising his intentions, she swiftly stepped backwards and disappeared behind the raspberry canes after aiming a parting jet of water at him and the hysterical Emily.

Max looked around for a weapon. Spotting Tom's giant water pistol from the other day, he filled it quickly at the scullery tap, then, motioning Emily to be quiet, they tiptoed around the soft fruit to try to sneak up on Thea.

Crouching down beside the raspberries Max took careful aim. He was rewarded by a startled shriek as the jet of icy water hit Thea firmly in the middle of her back. Emily's squeals of laughter alerted Thea to their whereabouts, and Max found himself embroiled in a full-scale water battle.

Finally, when all three of them were thoroughly drenched and he and Emily had wrestled the hose from Thea and squirted her till she'd begged for mercy, they collapsed in a giggling heap on the grass.

Eventually, when Thea had got her breath back, she sat up. 'I'd better find some towels, Emily's shivering.'

Emily got to her feet and extended her small hand to Max. 'Come on, Uncle Max.'

Standing up he picked Emily up and placed her on his shoulders where she swayed and clutched at his hair to keep her grip. 'Let's race Thea to the scullery!' he announced.

Jogging across the back lawn he was rewarded by Emily's whoop of delight as they got to the back door a step ahead of Thea.

Lifting Emily from his shoulders so that Thea could cocoon her in a warm dry towel, he took the opportunity to mouth a silent 'Thank you' to Thea.

Thea blushed and shook her head before throwing another towel to him and wrapping one round her own wet shoulders.

She couldn't understand Max's reservations about marriage and children. He would make a great dad. His love and care for his sister and little niece was so obvious, it had to be clear to him that he would be highly unlikely to repeat the mistakes his parents had made.

Absentmindedly she scrunched her hair dry with the towel while watching him help Emily to change her wet costume for a dry T-shirt and shorts.

As if sensing her eyes watching him Max looked up. 'Is everything OK? You look a bit pensive. Did we overdo the water?'

She shook her head. 'Don't be silly. It's such a lovely hot day a little cooling down was fine.'

'It was fun!' Emily piped up. Fully dressed now, she sat swinging her legs on one of Thea's pine kitchen chairs, her dark hair curling damply around her face.

'Well, I can see you've been busy baking. Who made these fantastic tarts?' Max leaned over and pretended to steal one of them.

'Me and Thea. We made picture pies of me, you and Thea,' Emily announced proudly and pointed out which pie was the picture of Max. 'You can eat that one 'cos it's you.'

Thea grinned as he admired the slightly grimy swirls of pastry which Emily had lovingly arranged on the jam tart.

'It looks wonderful. I think I'll eat it for supper.'

Emily beamed at him contentedly. 'Thea took photos and we emailed them to Daddy so he can show Mummy when she gets to Singingpore and she'll know I made them.'

'Clever Thea.' His gaze was warm with admiration, making her cheeks burn hotter than ever. She turned away to hide her embarrassment and the moment passed as Max went off to change out of his wet clothes.

★   ★   ★

The next few weeks seemed to fly past. There were some tears from Emily whenever she got overtired or particularly missed her parents, but Thea felt things were going well.

Julia and Paul emailed and phoned regularly, and from the snippets of conversation Max reported it appeared they were working through their problems.

Thea had become accustomed to having Max and Emily around the house and was dreading the time when they would have to leave. It felt as if she had a real family life again, the kind of life she'd always wanted. And although Max hadn't kissed her or made any kind of move towards her since Julia had gone, Thea knew the feelings were still there.

Why did she always have to pick the wrong man to fall in love with? One thing was certain, she needed to put a guard on her heart where Max was concerned or she was going to be left broken-hearted when he moved out.

Max, meanwhile, tried hard to convince himself that he was looking forward to moving out of Thea's home and her life once Paul and Julia were back. The past few weeks had been surreal, living in a family. At least, he supposed this was what a normal family life felt like — shopping, cooking, playing and enjoying Thea's and Emily's company, with none of the arguments, bitterness and devastating loneliness which had marred his and Julia's childhood.

He had always known he would miss Emily when the time came for her to return to her parents. What he hadn't been expecting was how much he was going to miss Thea. Being engaged to her seemed like the most natural thing in the world. He wondered sometimes if Ginny and Laurence had forgotten it was just pretend.

Everyone viewed them as a couple, inviting them out for drinks or dinner and talking as if he had moved permanently into Stony Gables. He'd even been asked about the autumn bazaar!

Emily was due to stay for another three weeks, then that was it. Paul and Julia would come home and he would be free to return to London and his bachelor lifestyle. He and Thea would say that they had found they weren't compatible after all and the fake engagement would be over.

He should have been happy, but he wasn't.

Then came the phone call from Julia: she and Paul were coming home early. They would be back at the end of the week and would be coming straight down to Stony Gables to collect Emily and take her home.

Emily was thrilled and ran about the house singing happily.

'This is it then, it's nearly over,' Thea said when Max told her. Her voice wobbled slightly.

'Julia said they'd managed to get a flight for Friday,' Max added, trying to tell himself this was a good thing.

Thea bit her lower lip and fiddled nervously with one of her earrings.

'I guess we should take Emily to Treetops then. We promised her we would before Julia came home.'

'OK, I think the weather's forecast to be good tomorrow. I'll square it with the office and we'll go.'

Thea watched him head back to the study, presumably to contact his colleagues. Two more days of pretending to be Max's fiancée, then Emily would leave, she would hand back the ring, Max would move out, and that would be that.

Max would probably be relieved. She wondered if he would contact Gabby again when he returned to London. The last she had heard from Ginny was that Gabby had decided that the country life wasn't for her and had given up her rented house.

Irritably she quashed the thought and decided to go up to Emily's room to start sorting out her things ready for her parents to collect her.

A pile of Emily's drawings was on the bedside table. Thea picked them up and began to leaf through them. Julia would probably like some of them to keep. There was a picture of Stony Gables, one of Peanut, her neighbour's little pony, and one captioned Thea and Max, which showed her with yellow hair to her feet wearing a wedding dress and Max with black hair. Tears sprang into her eyes and she buried her head in Emily's quilt and wept.

★   ★   ★

The next day dawned bright and sunny. Emily had heard so much about Treetops from Tom that she couldn't wait to go. She had a whole list of the attractions she wanted to visit.

'Promise we'll go to the petting zoo and the tree-house and the café with the talking parrots.' She chattered away excitedly, jumping up and down next to Thea as she packed drinks and sun cream.

'We'll have to wait and see,' Max warned, coming in behind them. 'That sounds an awful lot to see in just one visit.'

The queue to enter Treetops was already quite long by the time they reached the park. Max finally managed to park the car and they went to pay for the tickets.

'Isn't this great, Uncle Max? Mummy and Daddy would like it here, wouldn't they?' Emily skipped along happily between them.

'I'm sure they'll bring you here again when they get back,' Thea said, while stealing a peek at Max. He didn't look as if he was enjoying himself at all. She suspected it was probably the first time in his life that he had ever been to a theme park.

'Where are we going first?' He studied the plan of the park he'd been given with the tickets.

'The animals!' Thea and Emily answered in unison.

Max sighed, folded the map back up

and put it in his pocket. 'OK, the animals it is.'

They bought bags of animal food and made their way round the pens, petting and feeding the donkeys and goats and chickens.

'Isn't this like being at home for you?' Max murmured in Thea's ear as she bent to pet a rabbit.

'Isn't it fun?' Thea answered him. She was enjoying seeing the delight on Emily's face as the animals took the food from her hands.

'Fun?' Max looked bewildered.

Thea realised then just how out of his depth he was.

'Here, feed the goat,' she urged and tipped some feed into his hand.

'No, really — I don't want to.'

'Go on, Uncle Max, it's fun,' Emily urged. 'Here — I'll help . . . ' She clasped his wrist to guide his hand towards the goat's inquisitive tongue.

Thea watched as Max tentatively followed Emily's instructions. She knew it wasn't the feeding of the animals that he was finding so hard. It was the whole concept of a family day out. Taking pleasure in one another's company as a family was stirring long-buried emotions for him that he was struggling to deal with.

'See, Uncle Max? That wasn't so hard, was it?'

Little did Emily realise exactly how difficult her Uncle Max was finding this, Thea thought.

They made their way from the petting zoo to the tree-house, a long observation platform built high up in the trees by the lake aquarium where there were binoculars and telescopes to watch the animals.

Emily rushed forward to get a good space to watch the otter-feeding which was due to take place on the bank side.

'Are you OK with being here?' Thea murmured to Max once Emily was out of earshot.

'Truthfully, no. I don't know. It's just being here with Emily, playing the happy family . . . ' He ground to a halt and her heart went out to him. She doubted if he knew how to explain what he was feeling even to himself, let alone to her.

'Why don't you go and get a coffee? I'll stay here with Emily and we'll meet you later,' she suggested.

He glanced over to where Emily was impatiently waiting for them to join her. 'OK — I'll meet you in the café.'

He disappeared into the crowd and Thea went to join Emily with a bright smile fixed to her face and a heavy weight in her heart.

Emily looked around to see where he'd gone. 'Isn't Uncle Max going to watch the otters?'

'He's gone to get a drink, sweetie. We'll meet him in the café afterwards.'

'But he's missing all the good stuff,' Emily huffed, but then the keeper appeared with a bucket of fish and she was too busy craning for a better view to be cross for long.

The otter-feeding and talk lasted half an hour and Thea hoped that Max would be feeling better by the time she and Emily made their way to the jungle theme café.

The café was crowded since it was lunchtime and at first Thea couldn't see him. Rising fear gripped her as she held Emily's hand and scanned the room for his familiar figure. Then, to her relief, she saw him sitting in a far corner half hidden by a large animatronics gorilla family.

Thea and Emily pushed through the crowd to join him at his table. He looked tired, Thea thought.

'You missed the otters,' Emily said accusingly as she slid on to the orange plastic chair opposite him.

'I'm sorry, but hey, I got us a table for lunch.'

'Hmm.' Emily didn't sound convinced.

'Listen, talking of lunch, how about if I go and get us something to eat and you can tell Uncle Max about the otters?' Thea offered before Emily could start asking why he had missed the show.

'Can I have chips and nuggets?' Emily asked hopefully.

'I suppose so.' Thea smiled at her. 'I'll be back in a few minutes,' she added to Max.

By the time she returned with the lunch trays Max looked more like himself and was teasing Emily as he normally would.

They spent the rest of the afternoon on the various rides at the park, taking it in turns to ride with Emily on the flying elephants or the whirling teacups. Even so, Max was unusually quiet, but Emily was enjoying her day out too much to notice.

They stayed until it was almost time for the park to close, then, laden with a giant balloon and a huge bright blue stuffed cuddly dolphin, they headed for the exit. Emily struggled to stifle a yawn as she dawdled along the path to the car park.

'I think someone's tired. We'd better get you home and into bed,' Max observed.

'I'm not really tired!' Emily protested but before he had pulled out on to the main road, she was proved wrong.

'She's asleep,' Thea murmured, peeping through the rearview mirror to check on Emily.

'I'm not surprised. We must have walked miles around that place.'

'How are you feeling now?' Thea wasn't sure how to ask the question. She didn't want to sound as if she was probing.

'I'm sorry about what happened back there. It just got to me for a moment.'

She was silent for a moment while she pondered on what to say.

'Do you want to talk about it? You were very quiet this afternoon,' she said finally.

Max sighed and his shoulders tensed.

'I guess this trip crystallised some things for me. I can't do the family thing, Thea.'

'Can't or won't?' she challenged. 'I don't understand, Max. I know you and Julia had a terrible childhood and I know that it's left scars on both of you, but you're great with Emily. You would make a fantastic father.' And husband, she added silently to herself.

'I won't deny that the time I've spent with you and Emily has been fantastic, the best time of my life.'

'But?' she encouraged.

He didn't answer her, instead shaking his head, unable or unwilling to verbalise his feelings.

To Thea the message was perfectly clear. Whatever his feelings were for her, whatever she thought she'd read into his actions and words over the last few weeks, one thing was certain. He wasn't in love with her.

She was hurt, he could tell from the way her mouth had drooped and her eyes were sad as she gazed out at the scenery. He'd made such a hash of things. The last thing he'd wanted was to hurt a woman he'd come to admire and like so much. Any lingering doubts about Thea's motivations for helping him had been dispelled over the past few weeks. Although she might pretend it was all about the money to repair Stony Gables, he knew that she loved Emily.

He pulled the car on to the drive outside Stony Gables and went to lift the sleeping Emily from her seat while Thea unlocked the front door.

'Are we home?' Emily stirred as he carried her into the house.

'Yes, we're back.'

'I want Thea.'

Slightly surprised, he handed her into Thea's arms.

'Let's get you bathed and into your pyjamas,' Thea murmured.

Thea carried Emily off upstairs and Max went into the study to check for messages on the answering machine. There was one from his sister: 'We managed to get an earlier flight. I'm calling from the airport. Don't tell Emily and we'll surprise her tomorrow.'

He was pleased for Julia and Paul that they seemed happy again, but he had been thinking about how to make his last day with Thea count. How to put things right between them. He wished he could explain to her his fear that he would end up in a relationship like that of his parents, how he had almost made that mistake before. Leaving might hurt her now, but he would hurt her a lot more if he stayed.

Maybe he couldn't explain. Perhaps Julia and Paul returning tomorrow was for the best. They could collect Emily, he could wave them all off, pack his things and be back in his apartment tomorrow night.

* * *

Julia and Paul arrived late afternoon. Emily was playing on the swing in the garden. Thea was working in the garden, chatting to Emily as she swung. Max had been working in the study when he heard the car.

'Mummy! Daddy!' Emily leapt from the swing to race up the garden path towards her parents, Max watching from the patio with a lump in his throat.

Thea swallowed hard. Emily's joy at being reunited with her parents and their pleasure at reclaiming their daughter made her feel quite emotional. Julia looked radiant, a very different person from the fragile, emotional woman who had left only a few weeks ago.

'Thea, I'm so glad to see you. Come and meet Paul. I've told him all about you.'

Emily was in her father's arms and was hugging him for all she was worth while chattering nineteen to the dozen.

'You look so well and so happy, Julia,' Thea remarked, smiling.

Julia blushed. 'That's part of the news we didn't tell you over the phone. I'm having a baby.'

'You're pregnant? Oh, how wonderful!' Impulsively Thea hugged her.

'Emily's been wanting a brother or sister, and when she found out Tom was going to be a big brother, well ... ' Julia laughed happily.

'I guess this calls for a celebration. I'm sure I've got some wine in the fridge.' Thea linked arms with Julia and they walked back to the house.

She found the wine and some juice for Emily and Julia, and once the glasses had been handed round, she raised hers aloft.

'To Paul, Julia and Emily — congratulations and good health!'

She noticed that although Max was smiling his eyes were grave.

Julia had brought presents for them all, a watch for Max, a necklace for Emily, and when Thea opened her box she found a beautiful pair of earrings set with emeralds.

'Oh, Julia, thank you! But I can't possibly accept them.'

'Don't be silly! It's our way of thanking you for taking care of Emily. And they match your engagement ring so nicely,' she added with a smile.

Thea could feel her cheeks heating. She planned to hand her ring back to Max as soon as possible. She had a feeling he wouldn't be staying around Stony Gables once his sister had gone.

Emily had helped her to pack up all her things that morning and the suitcases stood ready to go in the tower bedroom.

Thea hated to think of how empty the house was going to be without her. Emily had helped her water the garden, collect the eggs and pet Peanut, the little pony in the neighbouring field. But lifting her head to meet Max's gaze, she knew beyond a shadow of a doubt that the person she would miss most was Max.

Paul carried Emily's case into the car while Emily hugged Thea hard.

'Mummy said you'll come and visit us with Uncle Max. Promise you will.'

Faced with the plea in Emily's voice Thea felt she had no choice but to agree. She would love to keep in contact with Julia and Emily but once the engagement was broken they might not want to see her again.

Thea waved till the car was out of

sight, grateful for Max's supportive arm around her.

'Are you OK?' he murmured.

She wiped a tear from her eye. 'I'll be fine in a minute. I'll really miss having her around. She's a great kid. I'm so happy for them though. It makes everything we've done seem worthwhile.'

Max nodded. 'You've been great, Thea. I couldn't have done this without you. Emily's her old self again and my sister is the happiest I've seen her in months.'

'I felt bad when Julia gave me the earrings. Which reminds me — I guess you may as well take this back now. There's no point in pretending any more.' She wriggled the engagement ring free from her finger and pressed it into his palm.

'No, don't. You should keep it,' he protested, and tried to give it back, but Thea stood her ground.

'No, it's yours. That was the deal when you bought it.' She tried hard to keep her tone even as if she were concluding some business deal, not surrendering all her secret hopes and dreams for the future.

'You must want the place back to yourself,' Max observed as they walked slowly up the drive towards the house.

Thea didn't trust herself to speak; he obviously wanted to leave as soon as possible. She shrugged her shoulders slightly.

'Well, it won't be long now,' he went on. 'I'm all packed and ready to go. I just have to finish packing some of the things in the study.'

'I see. Will you contact people and let them know — about us?'

'I'll sort everything out at my end. Ginny and Laurence will support you here.' He paused by the back doorstep. 'I hope we'll see each other again, Thea. Emily and Julia will want to see you.'

She couldn't look at him. She knew her eyes would betray the pain in her heart.

'I guess that's it then,' he said and disappeared into the house to finish packing.

Two Lonely Hearts

Max sighed and deleted the email from Julia. If she wasn't leaving him messages on his answering service she was lecturing him by email. He got up from his chair and walked heavily across the office to the window to look out over the busy street. It had been a week and a half now since he'd said goodbye to Thea. A small package of forwarded post stood on the corner of his desk, but there was nothing among it in her handwriting. He knew because he had checked.

The last ten days had been among the worst of his life. Leaving Thea at Stony Gables had been terrible. He had been checking his email, his post, his phone constantly ever since in case she got in touch. Yet why should she? He was the one who had left.

He stared sightlessly at the traffic. He'd done the right thing, he'd had to leave. Thea deserved someone who could give her the things she wanted — a happy family life, her happy ever after. He couldn't promise her that. He wasn't sure what he did have to offer her, except his heart, and he didn't know if that was enough.

★ ★ ★

'Thea, you were supposed to go down the snake.' Tom took her counter and moved it firmly down the board with an exasperated sigh.

'Sorry,' she apologised. Her mind wasn't on the game, it was somewhere else. It was wherever Max was.

'You're playing rubbish today,' Tom complained.

'I think you've won anyway, Tom. I'm right at the bottom and you're at the top,' she pointed out listlessly.

Ginny came into the conservatory just in time to hear Thea admit defeat. 'Has Tom beaten you again? That's not like you, Thea.'

The fine summer weather had broken and rain was drumming on the plastic roof of the conservatory. Thea had come over to amuse Tom while Ginny kept an antenatal appointment.

Ginny eyed her critically. 'Are you OK? You've lost weight.'

'I'm fine. I miss Emily. It's quiet without her.'

Ginny raised an eyebrow. 'Are you sure she's the only one you're missing?'

Thea felt the tell-tale traces of red steal into her cheeks. 'It was only ever a business arrangement between me and Max. You know that.'

'I know you fell in love with him, and he looked to me to feel the same way over you. According to Julia he's been as miserable as sin since he's been back in London.'

Thea shrugged. 'Leave it, Ginny, please. It wasn't meant to be.'

Ginny sank down on one of the cane chairs with a sigh. 'I think you're both as bad as each other.'

Thea stared glumly out of the

window at the rain. The ache in her heart was painful enough without Ginny mentioning Max's name. She knew her friend meant well, but hearing about Max was sweet agony. She had given up waiting for the phone to ring and ransacking the post every morning hoping for a message — anything that said he missed her, that he'd made a terrible mistake and wanted to come back.

It wasn't going to happen. Max wasn't the man for her, however painful it was to admit it.

Ginny was talking again. 'Julia wants you to visit them before you start the new job. She says Emily's desperate to see you.'

'I don't know. I'd love to see Emily, and Julia too, but — well . . . ' Thea trailed off, leaving the rest of the sentence unsaid. She knew Ginny would join the dots to work out why she would be reluctant to visit.

Ginny did. 'If you're worried about bumping into Max, don't be. Julia says he's snowed under with work. Every time she's invited him down lately he's made an excuse. She would have phoned you herself but she thought you might feel awkward.'

'I'll call her when I get home,' Thea promised. 'I would love to see them, and you're right, I'll be really busy next week when I start at the nursery.'

Ginny patted her hand sympathetically. 'I'm sorry it didn't work out with Max.'

Thea called Julia that evening. She felt guilty that she hadn't called before, but she had been unsure of what Julia's reaction might be.

In the event, she needn't have worried. Julia was delighted to hear from her and insisted that she visit at the weekend and stay for Sunday lunch, and by the time she came off the phone Thea felt confident that seeing Julia and Emily would put her one step nearer getting over Max.

★ ★ ★

Paul met Thea at the station early on the Sunday morning. All the way there Thea's stomach had been fluttering nervously. Suppose Max did turn up? Julia still had no idea that they had deceived her about the engagement.

Paul put her mind at ease straight away as they climbed into Julia's car.

'I'm glad you've come, Thea. Emily's missed you and Julia was worried that you might fear bumping into Max. Not that it's likely. Julia told him you were coming today but I think he's away for the weekend.'

Thea wasn't sure if she was relieved or disappointed. A tiny bit of her had been clinging to the hope that she might see him again.

Emily was waiting at the front door for her arrival.

'Come and see my bedroom, I've got lots of dollies, we can play tea parties.' She grabbed her hand and started to tug her towards the stairs.

'Hey, let her have a cup of tea first.' Julia laughed. Emily reluctantly stopped pulling but kept a tight hold of Thea's hand as Julia led the way to the sitting-room.

'Sit down, Thea. I'll go and fetch the tea.'

Thea sat down on the sofa and Emily jumped up to sit beside her.

'Mummy says you aren't going to marry Uncle Max.' Her dark eyes were accusing.

'No. Uncle Max and I decided it wouldn't be a good idea.'

'Don't you love him now?'

Thea wished life was that simple.

She was glad when Julia reappeared with a tea-tray. Julia spotted the slightly guilty expression on Emily's face straight away.

'Oh, Thea, I'm sorry! Has she been asking personal questions?'

'It's fine, Julia, really.'

Emily kicked her feet against the sofa. 'I didn't ask anything personal, Mummy. I only asked Thea if she loved Uncle Max.'

Julia raised her eyebrows. 'Heaven

help us if she thinks that's *not* a personal question.'

Emily folded her arms defiantly. 'I only wondered because Thea looks sad and Uncle Max is sad, too.'

Julia looked flustered. 'Emily, it isn't any of our business.'

Emily scowled. 'But you said . . . '

'Emily!' Julia said warningly and Emily subsided.

Thea accepted a cup of tea and chatted about her journey until Emily left the room to go and find a video she wanted to show her.

As soon as she was gone Julia apologised for Emily's outspokenness.

'I'm sorry, Thea. I know how painful this must be for you and Max. It's hard to understand. You looked so happy together.'

Thea swallowed. 'We just weren't suited, I guess.'

'For someone so smart my brother can be incredibly stupid.'

Thea fidgeted. She hoped Julia wasn't planning on using this meeting to urge her to reconcile with Max.

She could hear voices in the hall — the deep rumble of a man's voice mixed in with Emily's clear high-pitched tones.

The voices got nearer and Thea heard the words she'd been dreading: 'Come on, Uncle Max, Thea's having tea with Mummy.'

For an instant Thea thought she had been set up, but the shock on Julia's face showed that whatever else she may have been planning, she hadn't been expecting her brother.

The sitting-room door opened and there he was — Max.

'Hello, Julia — Thea.' He bent to kiss his sister's cheek then nodded at Thea before taking a seat in one of the armchairs.

'Max, I wasn't expecting you!' Julia shot to her feet. 'I'll just go and fetch another cup.' She hustled out of the room, shooing Emily before her, leaving Max and Thea alone.

Max looked tired, Thea thought, her

eyes drinking him in, trying to fix a picture of him in her mind.

'How are you?' she asked and wondered how she could sound so calm when her heart was thudding against her ribs.

'I've been better,' he said. His words took her by surprise.

'Julia said she wasn't expecting you today. Paul thought you were away for the weekend,' she said, aware that she was babbling.

'She wasn't.'

'Then why did you come?'

He gazed straight into her eyes. 'Why do you think?'

Her pulse was pounding and her hands were shaking. 'Max, please — don't play games with me.'

He crossed the room to sit beside her, taking her hands in his.

'I'm not playing games, Thea. I've come to realise over the last few days just what a prize idiot I've been and how I might have lost the most wonderful and special thing that's ever happened to me. I love you, Thea. I don't want to ever be without you.' He paused to gently wipe away a tear which threatened to run down her cheek. 'Tell me I'm not too late. I had a speech all prepared but it's gone. I guess I'll have to go with your famous 'wing it' plan.'

She sniffed and blinked, trying to hold back the tears.

'Thea, I know I've been a fool, but I've been doing a lot of thinking since we've been apart. I've been running scared of love for a long time. You were right when you said that, I was just too proud to admit it. I was scared I was going to end up like my parents and I didn't want that to happen to us, and to any children we might have. But seeing Julia and Paul work their problems out and being with you, I realised I'm not them. Thea, I love you. Will you marry me?'

She knew what it had cost him to finally admit his fears. Unable to speak for a moment, her throat choked with tears, she nodded. Then she was in his arms where she belonged. Tenderly his lips brushed hers, a sweet promise of their future together.

'See, Mummy, they're kissing. You won't have to bang their heads together now.' Emily had stolen back into the room and was smiling happily at them. 'Can I be a bridesmaid? I've got a pretty dress.'

★ ★ ★

The wedding took place at the village church eight weeks later. Laurence gave Thea away and Ginny and Julia were matrons of honour while Emily made a very pretty bridesmaid in a peach satin dress. Tom being Tom, he insisted that he wasn't going to be a ring bearer. Instead, he wore his suit with pride along with a pair of sunglasses, and told everyone that he was Thea's bodyguard.

Max thought he had never seen Thea look more beautiful than she did that day in a simple off-the-shoulder cream satin dress trimmed with moss green and her wild hair floating free under a circle of peach roses.

As the rose petals rained down on them at the lych-gate everyone remarked they had rarely seen a couple so much in love.

THE END

We do hope that you have enjoyed reading this large print book.

Did you know that all of our titles are available for purchase?

We publish a wide range of high quality large print books including:
Romances, Mysteries, Classics
General Fiction
Non Fiction and Westerns

Special interest titles available in large print are:
The Little Oxford Dictionary
Music Book, Song Book
Hymn Book, Service Book

Also available from us courtesy of Oxford University Press:
Young Readers' Dictionary
(large print edition)
Young Readers' Thesaurus
(large print edition)

For further information or a free brochure, please contact us at:
Ulverscroft Large Print Books Ltd.,
The Green, Bradgate Road, Anstey,
Leicester, LE7 7FU, England.
Tel: (00 44) 0116 236 4325
Fax: (00 44) 0116 234 0205

THE THEATRE ON THE PIER

Heather Pardoe

Escaping a disastrous relationship, Llinos Elliot moves to North Wales. There she gets a job as administrator with a children's community theatre, 'The Theatre on the Pier'. Llinos loves her job, and is drawn to Adam Griffiths, the artistic director. But she soon finds her past catching up with her, putting not only her and Adam, but the very existence of the theatre, in danger. Can Llinos overcome her past to find true happiness?

LOVE IN LAGANAS

Glenis Wilson

Maria Angelides, a trainee marine biologist, plans to visit the Greek island of Zakynthos, hoping to see loggerhead turtles, monk seals — and perhaps even the Greek father she has never known . . . Professor Nikos Cristol, an important visitor to the Marine Centre, offers to fly her to the island in his company plane. Enjoying the hospitality of the Cristol family, she becomes attracted to Nikos. But, confused by his intentions, will Maria really be able to find happiness with Nikos — or discover the truth about her father?

THE BROODING LAKE

Rosemary A. Smith

In 1890, Abbey Sinclair begins work as companion to Henrietta Kershaw at Kerslake Hall in Yorkshire. Abbey becomes attracted to both Mrs Kershaw's son Antony, and her nephew Thomas Craddock. She also befriends Alice, governess to Antony's daughter Emily. But many secrets lurk at Kerslake Hall. Who screams in the tower in the dead of night, and how did two women die in the brooding lake? Attempting to discover answers to these questions, Abbey is in danger of losing not only her heart, but her life too . . .

VALLEY OF DREAMS

June Gadsby

When Kelly Taylor divorces her husband, she decides to make a new start with her ten-year-old son, Alex, in the tiny hamlet of Labadette, in rural France. Alex becomes increasingly close to Jean-Paul Borotra, a shepherd — and their closest neighbour. But there is tragedy surrounding Jean-Paul and, despite the attraction she feels, Kelly holds back from developing their friendship further. And then, when Alex goes to visit his father in London, events take a frightening turn . . .

PASSION'S SLAVE

Rebecca King

Ramón Torres was accustomed to giving orders and having them obeyed. Those who wronged him, as Grant Leigh had, would feel his revenge . . . Georgia was wild and carefree, riding her motorbike down through Spain for her long-planned rendezvous with Grant, her beloved twin brother. But fate, in the form of Ramón, intervened. Even in her torment, something primitive stirred in Georgia, and Ramón knew it — just as he would always know everything about her . . .